"SCROOGE"

List of Drawings by RONALD SEARLE

PHOTOGRAPHS

"SCROOGE"

by Elaine Donaldson
Adapted From the Screenplay by Leslie Bricusse
Based on "A Christmas Carol" by Charles Dickens

CINEMA CENTER FILMS New York
AURORA PUBLISHERS, INCORPORATED Nashville/London

LIBRARY OF CONGRESS CATALOG CARD NUMBER: 71-1275
STANDARD BOOK NUMBER: 87695-085
MANUFACTURED IN THE UNITED STATES OF AMERIC

CONTENTS

MUSICAL NUMBERS
by
LESLIE BRICUSSE

THE CAST

Scrooge .... ALBERT FINNEY
Marley's Ghost .... ALEC GUINNESS
Ghost of Christmas Past .... EDITH EVANS
Ghost of Christmas Present.. KENNETH MORE
Nephew .... MICHAEL MEDWIN
Fezziwig .... LAURENCE NAISMITH
Bob Cratchit... DAVID COLLINGS
Tom Jenkins.. ANTON RODGERS
Isabel... SUZANNE NEVE
Mrs. Fezziwig.. KAY WALSH
Tiny Tim .... RICHARD BEAUMONT
Mrs. Cratchit .... FRANCES CUKA
Kathy .... KAREN SCARGILL
1st Gentleman of Charity .... DEREK FRANCIS
2nd Gentleman of Charity... ROY KINNEAR
Nephew's Wife .... MARY PEACH
Ghost of Christmas Yet To Come .... PADDY STONE
Nephew's Friend .... GORDON JACKSON
Toyshop Owner .... GEOFFREY BAYLDON
1st Woman Debtor.. MOLLY WEIR
2nd Woman Debtor .... HELENA GLOAG
Punch and Judy Man .... REG LEVER
Well-wisher .... KEITH MARCH
Party Guest .... MARIANNE STONE

It was Christmas Eve in London in the year 1860—a cold, bleak, foggy night. A carol service was in progress in St. Paul's Cathedral, and the words of a carol floated across the night air:

> *Sing a song of gladness and cheer,*
> *For the time of Christmas is here!*
> *Look around about you and see*
> *What a world of wonder*
> *This world can be!*
>
> *Sing a Christmas carol—*
> *Sing a Christmas carol—*
> *Sing a Christmas carol—*
> *Like the children do!*
>
> *And enjoy the beauty—*
> *All the joy and beauty—*
> *That a Merry Christmas*
> *Can bring to you!*

The spirit of Christmas was everywhere apparent: in the tumbling profusion of Christmas fare in the shop windows, in the happy, shining faces of children and their parents making last-minute forays for Christmas trees and holly and mistletoe from the greengrocer's shop, fresh-baked bread and plum cakes and Christmas puddings from the baker, plump turkeys and geese from the beaming butcher, and—best of all—presents from the glittering wonderland of the Christmas toyshops.

In Cheapside, the dulcet harmonies of the cathedral choir had given way to the strident cacophony of a group of scruffy street urchins, imploring mankind to " 'Ark the 'Erald Hayngels Sing." As the urchins bellowed, ". . . Peace on earf and mercy mi-hild . . ." a smiling well-wisher threw them a handful of copper coins from an upstairs window, calling, "There'll be no peace on earth with that bloomin' noise goin' on! Here you are, boys." As the coins jingled and bounced merrily on the cobblestones, the urchins scrabbled for them, and a brisk scuffle developed, rather detracting from the beauty of the moment!

One of the boys ran up some steps to a nearby doorway, assumed an angelic expression, and started to sing again, thumping loudly on the door as he did so. Beside the door a brass name-plaque gleamed dimly in the misty evening light. It read: "SCROOGE AND MARLEY. Private Merchant Bankers.

Moneylenders." The dark, chilly office contrasted strangely with the festive atmosphere outside in the street. It was business as usual there, though it was Christmas Eve and the evening was drawing in. Hunched at his desk, poring over his thick ledgers and some piles of sovereigns, sat Mr. Ebenezer Scrooge. There was no sign of the spirit of Christmas reflected in his hard, ungenerous features. He was as cold and bleak as the weather itself.

Scrooge looked up suddenly with an angry scowl as he heard the lusty sounds of the carol-singers outside. He slammed shut the ledger in which he had been writing, got up from his desk, and stomped towards the door, muttering sourly to himself, "Infernal horrible caterwauling. Why can't they leave a man in peace?"

He glared at his clerk, a young man in his early thirties who was sitting at a tall desk in the minute and dingy outer office. The clerk looked up as his employer passed, and Scrooge snapped, "Get on with your work, Cratchit!" Bob Cratchit's eyes returned at once to the ledger into which he was copying an interminably long column of figures.

Scrooge seized a thick walking-stick from the hat-stand and wrenched open the door violently.

Outside, the urchins smiled ingratiatingly. "Merry Christmas, guv'ner!" called one.

Scrooge raised his stick to strike them and roared, "Get away from here, you scavengers!"

Instinctively they scattered down the steps and ducked behind the railings. "Blimey, 'oo's 'e?" one of them asked.

"That's Farver Chris'mas!" replied his friend.

Angrily, Scrooge ran his stick along the railings and stamped at their hands with his foot. "A plague on Father Christmas!" he shouted.

The urchins dodged nimbly out of range. "An' '*e* sends 'is best to you, too, guv'ner!" With that they went rollicking off down the street, laughing raucously.

"Bah! Humbug!" roared Scrooge, slamming the door. "Insolent young ruffians, coming here with their Christmas nonsense . . . bah!" he muttered to himself, returning his stick to its place in the hat-rack. He glared again at Bob Cratchit, who was grinning broadly, and his glare instantly wiped the smile from the clerk's face. "Beware, Cratchit!" said Scrooge in a sinister tone. "You have a dangerous sense o' humour!" He wagged a long finger in Bob's face, and then moved on, still grumbling to himself.

Just as Scrooge reached his desk again, there came another pounding at the door, and a cheerful voice cried, "Merry Christmas, Mr. Scrooge!"

Scrooge was incensed, and as he turned round and crossed to the door again he roared his disapproval. "Hellfire and damnation! Don't they know I'm trying to run a business here?"

He grabbed his stick and flung open the door, but his wrathful reproaches died on his lips as he saw the charming, elegant, and smiling young man standing before him.

"Uncle Ebenezer," cried the young man, "I cannot tell you what a joy it is to see your happy, smiling face!"

"Oh! It's you!" growled Scrooge crustily, turning away from the door.

His nephew followed him jauntily into the office and closed the door. He gave Bob Cratchit a friendly nod and a wink and then said, "A Merry Christmas, Uncle Ebenezer! God save you!"

"God save me from Christmas! It's a lot of humbug!" snapped Scrooge, glaring. Swiftly and expertly he counted up a handful of gold sovereigns and dropped them into the money-box on his desk, slamming it shut to underline the sentiment. As he picked up the money-box and carried it over to the gigantic old safe, his nephew perched in a carefree fashion on the corner of the desk.

"Christmas a humbug? Come now, uncle, I'm sure you don't mean that!"

"And I'm sure I *do* mean that! Merry Christmas, indeed! What reason have you to be merry? You're poor enough!"

"And what reason have you to be miserable? You're rich enough!"

"There's no such thing as rich enough! Only poor enough!" replied Scrooge impatiently as he took an enormous bunch of keys from his watch-chain and unlocked the safe. The door creaked open. He rammed the money-box deep into the cavernous interior and slammed and locked the door with a clang.

"Don't be so dismal, uncle!" exclaimed his nephew.

"What else can I be, when I live in a world of fools babbling Merry Christmas at one another? To the devil with Merry Christmas! What's Christmas but a time for finding yourself a year older and not a day richer? There's nothing merry in that!" was Scrooge's angry rejoinder. He thrust his face menacingly at his nephew and growled, "If I could work my will, nephew, every idiot who goes about with Merry Christmas on his lips should be boiled with his own pudding and buried with a stake of holly through his heart!"

"Uncle!" protested the young man.

"You keep Christmas in your way, and let me keep it in mine!" replied

Scrooge sharply.

"But you don't keep it!" objected his nephew.

"Get off me ledger—you'll ruin me binding!" grumbled Scrooge. "Then let me leave it alone! And be good enough to leave *me* alone, sir, during business hours!" he went on.

Scrooge picked up the heavy ledger and examined the binding for possible damage. Scowling reproachfully at his nephew, he carried it across to a dusty bookcase to rejoin its fellows and locked it safely away with another key. As he did so, his nephew looked at his fob-watch. "Seven o'clock on Christmas Eve? That's not business hours! That's drudgery for the sake of it, and an insult to all men of goodwill!" he exclaimed.

At this, Scrooge's clerk muttered "Hear, hear!" under his breath.

"Thank you, Bob Cratchit!" said the nephew, bowing in good humour.

The smile vanished from Bob Cratchit's face as Scrooge emerged from the shadows and scowled at him. "Another word from you, Bob Cratchit, and you'll celebrate Christmas by losing your job!"

"Yes, sir. I'm sorry, Mr. Scrooge." Bob Cratchit licked his lips and returned to his letter-copying, breathing on his hands to keep them warm.

The nephew pulled a sour face behind his uncle's back, converting it into an instant smile as Scrooge turned to him, saying sarcastically, "You're quite a powerful speaker, sir. I wonder you don't go into politics—you're fool enough!" His nephew roared with laughter at this remark as Scrooge returned to his desk, straightened some papers on it, and then picked up another ledger even bigger than the first.

"Come now, uncle, don't be angry!" begged the young man. "Dine with my wife and me tomorrow!"

"As though you haven't got enough problems, you went and got yourself married! Now why in God's name did you ever do that?"

"Because I fell in love with the lady."

Scrooge opened the ledger with a growl. "Bah! If there's one thing in the world more nauseating than a Merry Christmas, it's the hypocrisy of a happy marriage with some lovesick idiot female! Good afternoon, sir!" He took up a quill pen and started to write in the ledger.

His nephew moved to the door, saying, "My offer stands. You are always welcome, uncle—just like Christmas itself!" Bob Cratchit sniggered.

"I said good afternoon!" was Scrooge's inexorable reply. He went on writing without looking up.

"I want nothing from you. I ask nothing of you. Why can we not be friends?"

"Good afternoon!" said Scrooge again.

"Merry Christmas, uncle."

"Good afternoon!"

"You too, Bob Cratchit! And your family!" added the young man, undeterred.

"Thank you, sir," said Bob with a smile. "And to your good lady!"

Scrooge's nephew departed, but a second later he popped his head round the door and called, with undiminished and provoking cheerfulness, "Oh, and uncle—a Happy New Year!"

"Good afternoon!" positively screamed the enraged Scrooge.

Grinning, his nephew went on his way, leaving Bob Cratchit considerably cheered up and warming his hands on the candle on his desk. Scrooge glowered at him. Bob smiled nervously, swallowed, and took his courage in both hands. "Excuse me, sir, but it's—er—seven o'clock, sir."

"Correct, Cratchit," replied Scrooge coldly.

"I don't wish to be impertinent, Mr. Scrooge, but will it be too much trouble if I have my wages, sir?"

"The trouble with you, Cratchit, is that all you think of is pleasure and squandering money." Scrooge took out his purse and carefully counted out fifteen shillings, inquiring as he did so, "You'll be wanting the whole day off tomorrow, I suppose?"

"If it's convenient, sir."

"It is not convenient, sir. And it is not fair. And yet if I stopped your wages for it, you'd think yourself ill-used, no doubt." Grudgingly he handed him the money.

"Thank you, sir. Well, sir . . ." stammered Bob nervously.

"And yet you don't think me ill-used when I pay a day's wages for no work."

"Well, it *is* Christmas Day, Mr. Scrooge. And it *is* only once a year, sir," said Bob apologetically.

"A poor excuse for picking a man's pocket every twenty-fifth of December! I don't pay good money for you to be forever on holiday!"

"I appreciate your kindness, Mr. Scrooge."

"That's my weakness—I'm a martyr to me own generosity! I give you one Christmas Day off and you expect 'em all! Very well, take the day. But be here all the earlier next morning!"

At this, Bob grabbed his long comforter from the hat-rack, wound it swiftly around his neck, and made hastily for the door before his employer could change his mind. "I will, sir. Yes, sir. Thank you, sir. And a Merry Christmas, Mr. Scrooge."

"Begone from here and take your infernal Merry Christmas with you!" thundered Scrooge.

"I mean, I beg your pardon, sir. No offence, sir," stammered Bob, scuttling quickly out of the door before the situation deteriorated any further.

As he watched his clerk go, Scrooge muttered to himself, "There's another one. Fifteen shillings a week, a wife and five children, and still talks about a Merry Christmas. Belong in a lunatic asylum, the lot of 'em!"

Outside in the street two small, ragged children, a little crippled boy and his sister, were waiting for their father. With shining eyes they gazed into the window of a toyshop, where a magnificent toy carousel revolved slowly as the musical box inside it tinkled out a happy tune. Behind it stood a glittering Christmas tree laden with toys and goodies. The children were spellbound, for never in their short lives had they seen such marvels.

Bob Cratchit joined his children and smiled rather wistfully as he saw them gazing so happily at the toys. "Kathy, my dear . . . Tim . . . oh, you're both frozen!" he exclaimed, embracing them fondly. "Sorry I'm late! Mr. Scrooge and I had a lot of last-minute business to attend to!" Pointing to the window full of toys he asked, "Well, my loves, which one do you like best?"

Kathy promptly pointed to a doll in the corner of the window, but Tiny Tim said, "I like all of 'em!"

"Good boy! And why not one in particular?"

"Well, you said I can't have none of 'em, so I might as well like 'em all!"

"Tiny Tim, you are a philosopher and a gentleman, and I've got fifteen shillings in me pocket which says the Cratchit family will have as good a Christmas as the Lord Mayor of London 'imself!" exclaimed Bob, kissing the little boy's face and lifting him up onto his shoulder. As they moved away from the window, Tiny Tim exclaimed in awe that his father should have so much money, and Kathy stole a last regretful look at the doll.

Bob and the children made their way home to Camden Town, and on the way they sang:

Christmas children peep into Christmas windows—
See a world as pretty as a dream.
Christmas trees and toys.
Christmas hopes and joys.
Christmas puddings rich with Christmas cream.

Christmas presents shine in the Christmas windows.
Christmas boxes tied with pretty bows.
Wonder what's inside—
What delights they hide.
But till Christmas morning no one knows.
Won't it be exciting if it snows?

I suppose
That children everywhere
Will say a Christmas prayer
Till Santa brings
Their Christmas things.

Christmas children hunger for Christmas morning.
Christmas Day's a wonder to behold.
Wondrous things to eat.
Every Christmas treat.
I believe that story we've been told.
Christmas is for children, young and old.

The streets were thronged with shoppers, many of whom were laden with expensive, brightly wrapped packages. On the way home Bob stopped to buy provisions for his family's Christmas dinner: a scraggy goose, the finest bird in the shop—for one and tenpence halfpenny; apples at six a penny (oranges cost too much); wine for making punch, at twopence a pint; and a Christmas pudding which cost the scandalous price of fourpence! He also spent a shilling on five little presents for the children, purchased from a street vendor dressed as Father Christmas.

When they got home, they and the packages were enthusiastically greeted by the other members of the family, who had been busy setting up their little Christmas tree. And the Cratchit family gathered round the tree to light their Christmas candles, in a spirit of love and contentment.

Meanwhile, Scrooge blew out the solitary candle that was the only lighting in his office. Wearing a high hat and heavy topcoat, he went out into the street, closed the door, and proceeded to lock, double-lock, treble-lock, and quadruple-lock his place of business with a further selection from the vast bunch of keys on his chain. Suddenly he became aware of two portly gentlemen standing behind him. He scowled suspiciously as they bowed to him, smiling.

"Have we the pleasure of addressing Mr. Scrooge, or Mr. Marley?" asked the first gentleman, indicating the brass plaque bearing the two names.

"It's no pleasure to me, sir, to be addressed by either of you, and Mr. Marley has been dead these seven years. Seven years ago this very night, he died."

"We have no doubt his liberality is well represented by his surviving partner," said the second gentleman.

Scrooge's eyes narrowed at the ominous word "liberality." "Liberality? Aha! Goodnight, gentlemen," he muttered hastily, setting off along the street, his hands thrust deep into his greatcoat pockets.

The two gentlemen scurried after him. "Mr. Scrooge, sir, at this festive season of the year, it is more than usually desirable that we should make some slight provision for the poor and the destitute," said the first.

"Excellent. Then I suggest you do so," replied Scrooge drily.

"You miss our point, sir," said the second gentleman. "The poor suffer greatly at the present time. Many thousands are in want of common necessaries."

Scrooge came to a halt and stared keenly at the two men. They were now standing outside a shop full of Christmas luxuries. "Are there no prisons?" he demanded.

"Indeed there are, sir. That's one thing there's no shortage of!" the first gentleman assured him.

"And the workhouses? Are they still in operation?"

"They are, sir, and I wish I could say they were not."

"The treadmill and the Poor Law are in full vigour, I trust."

"Both very busy, sir."

"I am very glad to hear it! For a moment I was afraid that something had occurred to stop them in their useful purpose!" He hurried on along the street.

The portly gentlemen pursued him. "Since these institutions scarcely furnish Christian cheer of mind or body to their unfortunate inmates, a few of us are endeavouring to raise a fund to buy the poor some meat and drink, and means of warmth. We choose this time because it is a time, of all others, when want is keenly felt, and abundance rejoices," the second gentleman explained. "What may we put you down for?"

"Nothing!"

"You wish to be anonymous?" asked the first.

Scrooge stopped again and glared at the two men. "I wish to be left alone, sir—that is what I wish. I don't make myself merry at Christmas and I cannot afford to make idle people merry. I have been forced to support the establishments I have mentioned through taxation—and God knows they cost more than they're worth! And those who are badly off must go there!"

"Many would rather die than go there!" protested the second gentleman.

"If they would rather die, then they had better do it, and decrease the surplus population! Goodnight, gentlemen!" snapped Scrooge caustically.

The two portly gentlemen, deflated and defeated, gave up the struggle. Scrooge walked away, muttering angrily to himself, "Humbug! Poppycock! Balderdash!" As he walked through a bustling street market thronged with cheerful people, he sang this nasty little song to express his philosophy of life:

> *Scavengers and sycophants and flatterers and fools!*
> *Pharisees and parasites and hypocrites and ghouls!*
> *Calculating swindlers! Prevaricating frauds!*
> *Perpetrating evil as they roam the earth in hordes!*
> *Feeding on their fellow men, reaping rich rewards!*
> *Contaminating everything they see!*

Corrupting honest men
Like me!

I hate people.
I hate people.
People are despicable creatures!
Loathsome, inexplicable creatures!
Good-for-nothing kickable creatures!
I hate people.
I abhor them.

When I see the indolent classes
Sitting on their indolent arses,
Gulping ale from indolent glasses,
I hate people.
I detest them.
I deplore them.

Fools who have no money spend it,
Get in debt, then try to end it!
Beg me on their knees befriend them,
Knowing I have cash to lend them!
Soft-hearted me! Hard-working me!
Clean-living, thrifty and kind as can be!
Situations like this are of interest to me.

I hate people.
I loathe people!
I despise and abominate people!
Life is full of cretinous wretches,
Earning what their sweatiness fetches—
Empty minds whose pettiness stretches
Further than I can see!
Little wonder
I hate people!
And I don't care
If they hate me!

He paused for a moment to steal a handful of roast chestnuts from a street vendor, and then drew a little black book from his pocket and scrutinized the contents closely. At this time of peace on earth and goodwill towards men

Ebenezer Scrooge was going to call on his debtors to demand the money they had borrowed from him. When they begged for a few more days in which to find the money, as Scrooge had known they would, he added more exorbitant interest to the sum they already owed him. He was quite deaf to the appeals of two elderly women stallholders and merely threatened to confiscate their stall unless they paid him within a week, causing the bystanders to mutter angrily. He also took a pair of socks without bothering to pay for them! As he walked away, he callously pushed aside a beggar woman carrying a child in her arms, snarling, "Bah!" Scrooge, oblivious of all concerns but his own, even went so far as to squeeze into the tent belonging to a Punch and Judy man. To the horror of the man working the little glove puppets, Scrooge demanded his money in ringing tones, and then stood up, disrupting the performance, to the great amusement of the watching children, and shook his finger threateningly in the man's face in an unconscious parody of Punch beating Judy with his stick.

It came as quite a disappointment to Scrooge when the tavern keeper presented him with all the money he owed him. He counted the sovereigns twice, but was finally forced to admit that the amount was correct. Tom Jenkins, the hot soup man, managed to buy another week's grace in paying his debt by promising Scrooge a free pot of broth every night for a year. In fact, he asked for *two* weeks as he handed Scrooge the soup, but Scrooge was adamant in insisting on only one week, though he did accept the proffered broth, which he took home with him.

Everywhere Scrooge went that night he spread fear, despair, and anger, but was himself untouched by the general merriment. And as he moved relentlessly from shop to shop, warmth, happiness, and cheer seemed to shrink away from the atmosphere of chilly gloom and emptiness which hung about the stooped, black figure like a pall. The very mention of the hated name of Scrooge caused laughter to cease, and when people smiled again, their eyes were clouded and their laughter seemed suddenly hollow. For Scrooge brought grim reality and the shadow of the workhouse to these people who had forgotten for a little while that they were poor.

But to him they were only so many names in his debt book, representing sums of money owed—untidy problems in his otherwise orderly life. Their poverty angered him because it caused him trouble. He felt no compassion for their suffering because he did not see it. He had no time for idle sentiment. Hard work was the only reality to Scrooge, and money his only love, and

he felt nothing but contempt and irritation at the folly he thought he saw around him. His heart was as hard and cold as the coins he hoarded so avidly.

Along his way, Scrooge again encountered the carol-singing urchins.

"Oh look, there's that lovable Farver Chris'mas again!" cried the first.

"Ah, bless 'is little stone-cold 'eart!

"On 'is merry way, no doubt, to bestow a Chris'mas kick on some penniless, crippled orphan!"

The fourth urchin turned on the others, imitating Scrooge. "Get away from 'ere, you scavengers!" he yelled.

At this they all roared with laughter, and trailed Scrooge at a safe distance, singing mockingly:

> *Father Christmas! Father Christmas!*
> *He's the meanest man*
> *In the whole wide world!*
> *In the whole wide world!*
> *You can feel it!*
>
> *He's a miser!*
> *He's a skinflint!*
> *He's a stingy lout!*
> *Leave your stocking out*
> *For your Christmas gift!*
> *And he'll steal it!*
>
> *It's a shame!*
> *He's a villain!*
> *What a game*
> *For a villain to play*
> *On Christmas Day!*
>
> *After Christmas*
> *Father Christmas*
> *Will be just as mean*
> *As he's ever been,*
> *And I'm here to say*
> *We should all send Father Christmas*
> *On his merry Christmas way!*

Scrooge finally rounded on the urchins, who scattered and, with ribald farewells to "Farver Chris'mas," went off in another direction.

CHAPTER 2.—MARLEY'S GHOST

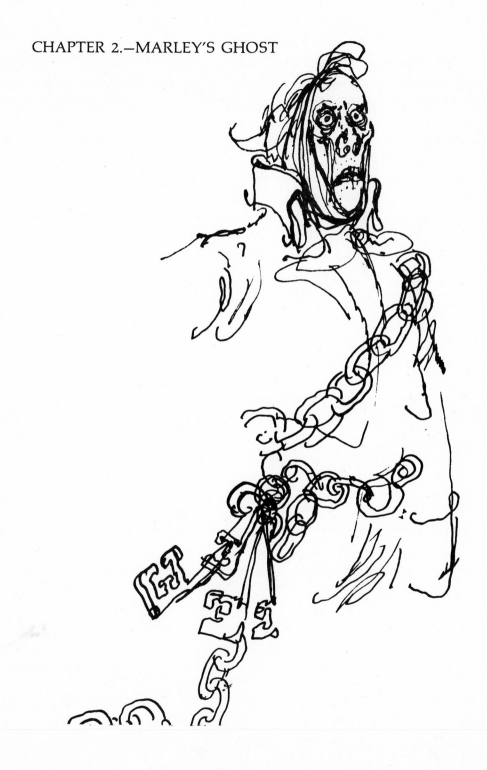

In the alleyway outside Scrooge's lodgings, an owl listened keenly as muffled footsteps crunched through the crisp snow. Suddenly it fluttered away with an alarmed "ter-whit-ter-whoo," as though recognizing the approach of Scrooge, whose shabby, stooped figure came through the swirling snowflakes into the ghostly pool of light cast by the solitary, flickering gaslamp.

Scrooge stepped into a dark doorway and in the gloom fumbled with his bunch of keys. He found the right one and placed it in the lock. As he looked up, the gargoyle head on the doorknocker turned into a human face. Glowing luridly, it stared at Scrooge and breathed his name in a deep, mournful voice: "Scroo-o-oo-ge . . ."

Scrooge was transfixed with terror. "Marley!" he whispered in horrified disbelief. Slowly the face faded, its voice repeating Scrooge's name in an eerie echo. Scrooge tried to pull himself together, muttering, "No! It can't have been! It's not possible! It can't have been!"

Nervously he turned the key in the lock and with some trepidation entered the house, keeping as far from the doorknocker as possible.

A sudden draught of air through the house caused the front door to slam behind Scrooge. Shaken, he turned slowly and looked at the back of the door—nothing! He bolted the door quickly. The sounds echoed and re-echoed through the large, sparsely furnished hallway, up the wide, sweeping staircase, and into the upper reaches of the old building.

His candlestick was waiting for him on a table near the door. With shaking hands he lit the candle and then made his way across the hallway. In the dim, flickering light, sinister shadows darted across the walls and ceiling as Scrooge started up the stairs. All at once he heard the sound of horses' hooves, and as he looked down he gave a stifled cry, for he seemed to see a phantom hearse driving across the hall. As it disappeared silently through the bolted front door, its ghostly driver raised his hat in greeting to Scrooge, who was standing rooted to the spot with fear. As he stood there trembling, he thought he heard the echoes of ghostly laughter in the distance. He groaned.

Then he hurried on up the stairs, the sharp sound of his shoes on the bare floors echoing through the house. The noise made him quicken his step, and as he went faster, so the volume of sound increased. By the time he ran into his sitting-room and slammed the door, the entire house was reverberating with the deafening echoes of a thousand running footsteps.

Breathing heavily, Scrooge leaned against the door, listening to the retreating waves of sound. When at last total silence prevailed, he let out a long

sigh of relief and walked across to the fireplace, unbuttoning his greatcoat and still muttering to himself, "It's not possible! Not possible!"

A mean fire smouldered in the grate, and he set the pot of soup on the hob to simmer. Beside it, a spoon and basin were set out ready for him. A mournful wind moaned in the chimney, and Scrooge remained ill-at-ease. He crossed to a wardrobe in the corner, hung up his hat and coat, and then went back to the fireplace. He pulled his old wing-backed armchair close to the hearth to make the most of the scant heat from the miserable fire. Then he poured the broth into the bowl and settled back into his chair to enjoy it.

As he raised the first spoonful to his lips, his hand started to shake uncontrollably, slopping the broth back into the bowl and into his lap.

In the chimney the wind howled and seemed to call his name: "Scroo-o-o-ooge!"

Scrooge stared, wild-eyed, as a bell beside the fireplace in front of him slowly started to swing. At first it made scarcely a sound, then it gathered strength, swinging wildly back and forth, and other bells rang all through the house, filling the night with strange sounds. Scrooge put down his bowl of broth and clapped his hands over his ears as the bells reached a deafening crescendo.

Suddenly there was total silence. Scrooge's eyes darted suspiciously from side to side. He took his hands from his ears and listened intently.

Then he heard a deep, hollow clanking sound and heavy footsteps far below. He put his ear to the floor, and at once the noise grew louder and more distinct. Reverberating echoes of dragging chains, creaking doors, dismal wailing, and muffled footsteps mingled together in a mounting nightmare of sound. Scrooge rushed to the door. The noise was coming up the stairs, growing louder at every step. Scrooge bolted and double-locked the door and hurried back to his chair, peering round it in mortal dread.

He watched, appalled, as the bolts of the door slid silently back and in the lock the key turned, once, then again, without the aid of any human hand. Then he gave a cry of sheer terror as the door flew open and a great rush of icy air blew across the room. In the doorway stood the ghost of Jacob Marley.

"Ebenezer Scrooge!" said the apparition, walking slowly towards him. The door shut itself again. The bolts slid back into place, and the key turned twice. Scrooge was locked in with the ghost.

Scrooge leapt to his feet and cowered back against the fireplace, too terrified to move further as he confronted the shade of his former partner. In a voice that was a hollow whisper of disbelief, he gasped, "Marley!"

Marley was swathed in a great chain made up of cash-boxes, ledgers, keys, padlocks, deeds, and heavy purses. It weighed down his semi-transparent figure. It dominated him. He gazed at Scrooge with death-cold eyes.

Scrooge gulped but rallied. "H-how now! What do you want with me?" he demanded.

"Much!" was the reply.

"Who are you?"

"Ask me rather who I was."

"Who *were* you then?"

"In life I was your partner, Jacob Marley."

"Can you sit down?" asked Scrooge.

"Of course I can sit down."

"Do it, then."

The ghost subsided into a sitting position in mid-air, with much clanking and evident relief. "You don't believe in me, do you?" he asked.

"No," replied Scrooge, "I don't."

"Why do you doubt what you see?"

"Because I've had a slight stomach disorder. It has undoubtedly affected my vision. You are an hallucination, probably brought on by an undigested bit of beef, or a blob of mustard, or a crumb of cheese, or an old potato! Yes, that's what you are—you're an old potato! I tell you, Marley, there's more of gravy than of grave about you! You do not exist, Jacob Marley! Humbug, I tell you—humbug!"

Gaining confidence, Scrooge picked up his bowl and again raised the spoon to his lips. Marley leapt to his feet with an agonized cry, shaking his chain and making an appalling noise. Then he floated up to the ceiling. Scrooge started nervously and dropped the bowl, which shattered on the hearth.

"Stop! I beseech you, stop!" he cried, falling to his knees before the phantom and clasping his hands in front of his face.

The phantom promptly stopped and resumed his seat, inquiring as he did so, "Now do you believe in me?"

Scrooge nodded, and then shook his head, in simultaneous assent and bewilderment. "I believe in you! Absolutely!" he said. Then, after a slight pause he asked, "But why do you walk the earth? And why do you come to persecute me?"

In a deep and mournful voice Marley replied, "Sooner or later, the spirit of every man must travel among his fellow men. If it does not choose to do so freely during his life, then it is condemned to do so after his death. Doomed to wander through the world—oh, woe is me!—and witness what it can no longer share, but might have shared in life, and turned to happiness!" Again the ghost uttered a desolate cry and shook his chain, as though overwhelmed with remorse.

Trembling, Scrooge asked, "What is that great—er—chain you bear?"

"I wear the chain I forged in life, by my misdeeds to my fellow men. I made it link by link, and yard by yard. I girded it on of my own free will during my life, and now I can never be free of it. Any more than you will ever be free of yours."

"Mine?" faltered Scrooge, trembling still more.

"Can you imagine the weight and length of the mighty coil you are making for yourself?" asked Marley. "It was full as heavy and as long as this seven Christmases ago! You have laboured incessantly on it since, and added some impressive new links to it! It is a ponderous chain you are constructing, Scrooge."

Scrooge instinctively looked about his person for the chain, and was relieved to find that it was not there. "Jacob! Old Jacob Marley, tell me more!" he pleaded. "Speak comfort to me, Jacob!"

"I have none to give! Comfort comes from other sources, Ebenezer Scrooge, and is conveyed by other ministers than I to other kinds of men than you. Nor can I tell you all I would. I cannot stay. I cannot linger anywhere. When I lived, my spirit, like yours, never walked beyond the narrow limits of our counting-house. And now no degree of regret can ever make amends for life's opportunities misused!"

"But you were always a good man of business, Jacob."

"Mankind is our business, Ebenezer. But how seldom we attend to it! Come. You shall see."

"What? Where?" cried Scrooge in alarm.

Marley moved towards the window, beckoning Scrooge to follow. Scrooge shook his head unwillingly, but followed anyway.

"How it is that I appear before you in a shape that you can see, I may not tell," said Marley. "I have sat invisible at your elbow many and many a day in your office."

Scrooge shivered at the thought. As they approached the big window it opened wide. So did Scrooge's eyes.

"Yet I must take this chance to warn you," Marley continued. "It is your only hope."

Before Scrooge could object, Marley threw a loop of his chain over his former partner's arm and, thus linked together, they sailed out through the window. Scrooge cried out in alarm.

The sky was filled with phantoms, ghostly figures like Marley, fettered like him with the appropriate symbols of their lives, and all of them seeking like him to overcome the remorse that would never leave them. They could see the poor and the destitute whom they had once had the power to help, but had, instead, neglected. Now they wanted to help them, but no longer had the power. It was too late.

Marley led Scrooge through this ghostly fantasy, explaining to him something of the torments men feel about the things they might have done to help others, but didn't. With deep gloom, Marley sang:

See the phantoms
Filling the sky around you!
They astound you,
I can tell—
These inhabitants of Hell!
Poor wretches
Whom the hand of Heaven ignores—
Beware! Beware! Beware!
Lest their dreadful fate
Be yours!

Make the most of this world!
The next world is worse!
If you think life is miserable now,
But the life to come is better somehow,
You'd better put all your thinking in reverse
And make the most of this world—
For the next world
Is far, far worse!

Make the most of this life!
The next life's a curse!
The man who kicks the present aside
In a quest for things life doesn't provide

Had better know now his theory is perverse
And make the most of this life—
For the next life
Is far, far worse!

Let's talk about Heaven a minute—
Men dream of it from birth.
Heaven—you idiot—
You're in it
On earth!

So make the most of living—
For dying is worse!
At times you'll say life isn't worthwhile
But there's more to life than travelling in style!
It's better to walk than ride inside a hearse!
So make the most of this world!
Embrace the universe!
For I guarantee
The next world
Is far, far worse!

Scrooge awoke to find himself sitting in his wing-backed armchair. He listened. All was quiet.

"It was a dream!" he exclaimed, smiling with relief.

"It wasn't a dream, Scrooge," said Marley's voice.

Scrooge jumped from his chair with a start. Marley's ghost was sitting in the other armchair, facing him.

"For pity's sake, Marley, leave me in peace!" cried Scrooge.

Marley rose slowly to his feet. "It was for pity's sake that I came here. Pity for you!" he said. "I must leave you now, Scrooge. But I leave you with a chance and hope of escaping my fate!"

At this, Scrooge looked slightly cheerful for the first time since meeting the apparition. "You were always a good friend to me, Jacob," he said. "Thank you."

"You will be visited by three spirits," continued Marley.

Scrooge's cheerfulness departed instantly. "Is that the chance and hope you mentioned, Jacob?" he inquired.

"It is."

"I—I think I'd rather not, if it's all the same to you."

"Without them, you cannot hope to avoid the fate of Jacob Marley."

"Ah, I see."

"Expect the first tonight when the bell tolls one."

"Couldn't I take 'em all at once, and get it over with?" asked Scrooge hopefully.

"The second will appear to you at two, and the third when the bell tolls three. Look to see me no more."

"Now, Jacob, just a minute—"

"For your own sake, look that you remember what has passed between us!"

"Marley, wait!" cried Scrooge.

"Farewell, Scrooge! Pray for me!" Marley raised his arm as his voice and his form faded into nothing.

Scrooge looked round the empty room—at the broken bowl upon the hearth, the stilled bell, the closed window, the locked and bolted door. "Pray for me, too!" he said.

He lit a candle and carried it towards another door on the far side of the room. Both Scrooge and the candle were shaking. Nervously, he peered round the door into his bedroom. When he was reassured that the room was empty, he walked slowly across it towards his curtained four-poster bed, deep in thought. He removed his outer garments, putting a nightshirt over his long winter underwear. He put on his nightcap, bedsocks, and slippers. Then he wound and set the alarm clock on the table beside the bed. It was midnight. Finally he kicked off his slippers and clambered into bed, drawing the curtains on two of the three open sides. He paused before closing the curtains at the foot of the bed.

"Three spirits?" he muttered. "Bah! Three humbugs!" He closed the curtains with a fierce tug, put out his candle, and settled down to sleep.

As he slept, confused thoughts and fantasies tumbled through his mind. He imagined himself gradually weighed down, strangled, and eventually buried by a massive chain of money-boxes, keys, and other symbols of his life. Marley's face was everywhere in the dream.

CHAPTER 3.—THE GHOST OF CHRISTMAS PAST

Scrooge's dream was suddenly shattered by what sounded like the knell of doom. With a deep, melancholy boom, the church clock struck one.

A light flashed on in the bedroom, and a pair of hands grasped the curtains at the foot of the bed and drew them aside.

Scrooge sat bolt upright in bed with a startled cry, staring at the imposing figure that confronted him. Beside him stood an elderly lady—a lady of quality, very dignified and distinguished looking. She was clad in a long red dress and on her white hair she wore a large feathered hat. Her manner was that of an eternal grandmother, kind, but very firm. At first, Scrooge was so frightened that he could not speak, and he tried to calm down a little before trying to address the apparition.

"Who-who-who-who . . ." stammered Scrooge at last, removing the pompom of his nightcap from his eye.

"I am the spirit whose coming was foretold to you."

Scrooge began to get a grip on himself, but his voice still quavered as he said, "You don't . . . *look* like a ghost."

"Thank you."

"Er—may I inquire more precisely who or what you are?"

"I am the Ghost of Christmas Past."

"Long past?"

"No. Your past."

"And what business brings you here?"

"Your welfare."

"To be woken by a ghost at one o'clock in the morning is hardly conducive to my welfare!" observed Scrooge peevishly.

"Your redemption, then. Take heed!"

Scrooge gasped with fear and recoiled as the ghost reached out and touched his arm.

"Rise! And walk with me!" commanded the ghost.

"I am really in no mood to go for a walk. It's too cold, and besides, I'm in my nightclothes!" protested Scrooge, as the vice-like grip of the ghost removed him gently but firmly from his bed.

But there was no resisting the ghost. They walked towards a blank wall.

"Where are we going?" asked Scrooge.

"Through the wall."

"That may be all right for you, but I am a mortal, and I do not walk through walls!"

"Bear but a touch of my hand and you will walk through anything!"

"But I don't want to go out again!" objected Scrooge. "I've just been out with Marley, and it's freezing cold, and I . . . oh dear! . . ."

They walked through the wall. Scrooge winced in anticipation of the impact, but there was none.

Scrooge and the ghost were standing on an open country road. It was a crisp, clear winter's day. The city had entirely vanished. Snow covered the fields on either side of them, and draped the trees with lace.

A look of recognition came into Scrooge's eye, distant at first, but growing as every glance sparked his memory. "I know this place!" he cried. "I was born here! In the little house—where is it?" He spun round, searching, and put his arm round the ghost's shoulders as he pointed. "Over there! That's it! That house there!"

A small but pretty Queen Anne house nestled in a copse of trees on the rise of a hill nearby.

For the first time, there was a glimmer of human warmth in Scrooge's eye as the contentment he felt in these familiar surroundings reached him. He looked at the ghost in wonder, exclaiming, "I was a boy here! I was happy!"

"Here come some of your boyhood friends—they're going to a Christmas party in the town!" said the ghost.

Along the road came a motley cavalcade of gigs and carts and pony-traps and farm vehicles bearing the local children to the town. The children were in rollicking high spirits, and singing a carol as they paraded past like a phantom carnival in the snow. This was the carol they sang:

> *Sing a song of gladness and cheer,*
> *For the time of Christmas is here!*
> *Look around about you and see*
> *What a world of wonder*
> *This world can be!*
> *Sing a Christmas carol—*
> *Sing a Christmas carol—*
> *Sing a Christmas carol—*
> *Like the children do!*
>
> *And enjoy the beauty—*
> *All the joy and beauty—*
> *That a Merry Christmas*
> *Can bring to you!*

Scrooge recognized the children and waved to them, but they did not see him. Enchanted, he even sang a few lines of the carol. Excitedly he cried, "I remember them! All of them! They look just like they did all those years ago!" He noticed his little sister, Fan, in one of the carts, and called out to her. He was puzzled when she did not respond.

"She cannot see you," explained the ghost. "These are but shadows of the things that have been."

"I could never join in those Christmas parties," remarked Scrooge sadly. He was deeply moved by this glimpse into his childhood.

"Your lip is trembling," observed the ghost. "And what is that upon your cheek?"

Scrooge hastily wiped away the tear with the pompom of his nightcap and restored his usual surly expression, muttering, "This infernal cold weather. Makes the eyes water."

The moment of sentiment had passed, and Scrooge was his normal irritable self again as he snapped, "Well, what have we come here for? To freeze to death?"

"We are going to look at some of the Christmases of your life," replied the ghost calmly. "We start from here. Come!"

The ghost took Scrooge's arm, and the unlikely couple set off along the road together.

"But I don't want to see the Christmases of my life! Any of them!" grumbled Scrooge. "What good has Christmas ever done me?"

"You used to enjoy Christmas—until you were sent away to that school."

"What school? Oh, yes."

"This school," said the ghost.

They were standing outside a depressing redbrick mansion. Scrooge looked at it with distaste. "The school is not quite empty, is it?" asked the ghost gently. "A solitary boy, neglected by his family, is left there still."

Now they stood inside a long, bare, melancholy schoolroom, made barer still by lines of plain, deal forms and desks. At one of these a lonely boy was reading near a feeble fire. From time to time he gazed into the fire, lost in daydreams.

Scrooge sat down upon a form and wept to see his forgotten self as he used to be. "Poor boy!" he cried, filled with pity for his former self.

Then he put his hand in his pocket. "I wish . . ." He looked about him and dried his eyes with his cuff.

"What is it?" asked the ghost.

"Nothing. Nothing," said Scrooge hastily.

"What do you wish?"

"There were some boys singing a Christmas carol at my door last night. I should like to have given them something, that's all." He looked sadly at his former self.

The Ghost of Christmas Past smiled thoughtfully. "Let us look at another Christmas," she said.

Scrooge looked at the ghost and then glanced anxiously back towards his young self.

Ebenezer, now a few years older, was sitting in the same place. The door opened and a little girl came in—the one Scrooge had called to as the procession passed by. She, too, was older. She flung her arms round the boy and kissed him fondly, crying joyfully, "Ebby, dear, dear brother, I have come to bring you home!"

"Home, little Fan?" asked the boy.

"Father is so much kinder than he used to be," she explained. "He sent me in a coach to bring you home, Ebby. We'll be together all Christmas long. Go and fetch your things."

As Ebenezer moved round the schoolroom collecting his few possessions, the ghost observed, "Always a delicate creature, whom a breath might have withered. But she had a large heart."

"So she had, I'll not deny it," replied Scrooge.

"She died a woman, and had, I believe, children," continued the ghost.

"One child."

"Your nephew!"

"Yes. . . ." said Scrooge uneasily.

The ghost was looking off into the distance. "Now there's a Christmas you really enjoyed!" she exclaimed.

"Where?"

"There!" said the ghost, pointing ahead.

Scrooge looked, and immediately his face brightened.

In the office of a warehouse, a fat, jolly, middle-aged gentleman was sitting at a desk so high that his head was almost touching the ceiling. He looked at the clock in front of him, roared with laughter, and rubbed his hands with delight.

"It's old Fezziwig! Bless his heart!" cried Scrooge. "I was his apprentice!"

Fezziwig clambered down the side of his high chair, which was practically a ladder, still chuckling to himself. Scrooge and the ghost stood watching, unseen by Fezziwig, who beamed round his office as he adjusted his capacious waistcoat, and called out in a rich, jovial voice, "Ebenezer! Dick!"

Scrooge's former self, now a young man in his twenties, came briskly into the room, accompanied by his fellow apprentice.

Scrooge nudged the ghost. "My word, I *was* handsome! And that other fellow, I remember him! Dick Wilkins! Nice young fellow! Very attached to me, he was. Dear, oh dear!"

"No more work tonight, my boys!" cried Fezziwig. "Christmas Eve, Dick. Christmas, Ebenezer! Let's have the shutters up before a man can say Jack Robinson! Clear everything away and make some room here before Mrs. Fezziwig and me daughters arrive with the punch bowl!"

Ebenezer and Dick leapt into action; Fezziwig hurled coals on the already roaring fire and scuttered up and down his chair-ladder, chuckling merrily; and the office and warehouse were transformed in an instant from a place of business into a party setting.

Old Scrooge was so delighted at this memory that he instinctively joined in and tried to move some furniture out of the way to help. But he was a ghost, and his hands moved through everything he tried to touch, for he had no substance.

The door burst open and Mrs. Fezziwig erupted into the room. She had brought the entire party with her—food, drink, decorations, guests, and music. Everybody was carrying something, and within seconds there were thirty or forty people in the room. Fezziwig greeted his wife with a smacking kiss, and then, holding up his hand for silence, he announced that there would be happiness and contentment in the room, the like of which none of them had ever seen before. At this the fiddler struck up a jig, and to a roar of approval from the company, old Fezziwig launched into the first dance with his lady, who was every bit as fat and jolly as he was. The rest of the company promptly joined in, and the warehouse positively resounded with merriment. As they danced, they all sang this song in celebration of Christmas:

Of all the days
In all the year
That I'm familiar with—
There's only one
That's really fun—
December the twenty-fifth!

Ask anyone called Robinson
Or Brown or Jones or Smith
Their favourite day
And they will say—
December the twenty-fifth!

December the twenty-fifth, me dears.
December the twenty-fifth.

The dearest day in all the year—
December the twenty-fifth!

If there's a day in history
That's more than any myth—
Beyond a doubt
One day stands out—
December the twenty-fifth!

I don't hear any arguments
So may I say forthwith
I wish that every day could be
December the twenty-fifth!

December the twenty-fifth, me dears.
December the twenty-fifth.
The dearest day in all the year—
December the twenty-fifth, me dears.
December the twenty-fifth, me dears.
December the twenty-fifth, me dears.
December the twenty-fifth!

"What a marvellous man!" cried Scrooge, punching the ghost's arm enthusiastically.

The ghost winced and asked, "What's so marvellous? He has merely spent a few pounds of your mortal money—three or four perhaps. What is that to be deserving of so much praise?"

Scrooge looked at her disapprovingly. "You don't understand," he said. "He has the power to render us happy or unhappy—to make our work a pleasure or a burden. It's nothing to *do* with money! This happiness he gives is as great as if it had cost a fortune!" Without knowing it, he spoke like his younger self. Then Scrooge saw the ghost looking at him knowingly and stammered, "He—I . . ."

"What's the matter?"

"Oh, nothing," replied Scrooge. "I was just thinking about Bob Cratchit."

"Who's Bob Cratchit?"

"No one," said Scrooge hastily. He dismissed the matter from his mind and turned his attention back to the festivities around him.

The fiddler was controlling the operation from atop Fezziwig's lofty desk, and the warehouse was now a whirl of dancing figures. Only Ebenezer did not join in the dancing. The ghost pointed to the lonely figure watching the dancers and asked, "Why didn't you join in the dance?"

"Because I couldn't do it," replied Scrooge after an embarrassed silence.

Watching Ebenezer was the younger and very pretty Miss Isabel Fezziwig. Scrooge caught his breath when he saw her and gasped, "Isabel!"

"Fezziwig's daughter," said the ghost. "You were going to marry her, weren't you?"

"Yes. . . ." replied Scrooge abstractedly. He could not take his eyes off Isabel, who was inviting his younger self to dance.

Ebenezer was acutely shy, but with a warm, reassuring smile Isabel gently coaxed him away from his place by the wall and onto the floor to join the other dancers. He danced very badly, but Isabel nodded encouragingly. Scrooge smiled wistfully as he looked at them.

Scrooge and the ghost watched as the happier days of his youth unfolded before them. They saw Isabel, who clearly adored Ebenezer, trying with great love and understanding to bring him out of his shell and introduce him to a world of pleasure and happiness that his many inhibitions made it hard for him to accept. Isabel was always gay and spontaneous, full of joy and laughter. Ebenezer was nervous and self-conscious, ill-at-ease and preoccupied. But they were happy days, even though he was an inexpert punter and even worse at archery! Golden, idyllic days in the country with the girl he loved and who loved him.

Finally, Scrooge watched the two young people driving home one glorious evening at sunset. With considerable awkwardness, Ebenezer took Isabel's hand and slipped a very slim, not to say mean, silver ring on her finger. The happy Isabel smilingly pointed out that he had put it on the right finger, but the wrong hand. With an even greater display of clumsiness, he corrected his error and then kissed her cheek modestly. Isabel snapped the reins and the pony picked up speed. Then she looked lovingly at Ebenezer, leaned over, and kissed him. Their happiness seemed complete.

And as he watched, Scrooge heard again the voice of Isabel singing:

> *They say happiness is a thing you can't see,*
> *A thing you can't touch.*
> *I disagree.*
> *Happiness is standing beside me.*
> *I can see him. He can see me.*
> *Happiness is whatever you want it to be.*

Happiness is a high hill.
Will I find it? Yes, I will.
Happiness is a tall tree.
Can I climb it? Watch and see.

They say happiness is the folly of fools.
Pity poor me, one of the fools.
Happiness is smiling upon me,
Walking my way, sharing my day.
Happiness is whatever you want it to be.

Happiness is a bright star.
Are we happy? Yes, we are.
Happiness is a clear sky.
Give me wings and let me fly.
Let me fly.
For happiness is whatever you want it to be.

Scrooge looked wistfully at the ghost. "I did love her, you know," he said.

"Did you?"

"Oh, yes. I loved her."

"But you let her go."

Scrooge smiled in sad bewilderment. "Yes. I've never been quite sure why."

"Let's have a look and see."

Then Scrooge saw himself as a slightly older man, no longer an apprentice, but a well-to-do young man of business. He was sitting at his desk, engrossed in work, as Isabel knocked and came into the office. The old Scrooge and the ghost stood by the desk, watching. Scrooge again studied his younger self intently.

As they talked, Isabel tidied up the office, replacing the faded flowers on the desk with the fresh ones she had brought with her, slowly and quietly putting things straight, arranging scattered papers into neat piles—little touches here and there that effortlessly transformed the office, as effortlessly as Isabel had once transformed Ebenezer.

"Ebenezer?" said Isabel.

"Mmmmmm?" murmured Ebenezer, not looking up from his work. Isabel stood by his desk, looking at him with tears in her eyes.

Old Scrooge stood right beside her, and now looked at her with a sadness greater than her own. He shook his head forlornly.

"I have come to say good-bye," said Isabel.

"Mmm?" said Ebenezer again.

"I am going away," she continued.

"Mmmm."

"You will not see me again."

"Listen to her, you fool!" cried Scrooge to his younger self.

Slowly Ebenezer looked up at Isabel as her words penetrated. "But you are going to marry me!"

Isabel shook her head, and removing the engagement ring from her finger, she said, "No. You have found another love to replace me—and she is much more desirable than I am."

"I have no idea what you're talking about," replied Ebenezer slowly.

Isabel put her hand into the open money-box on the desk and let a handful of gold sovereigns trickle through her fingers as she said, "This lady here."

Ebenezer put down his pen and looked at the gold, and then at Isabel. "How shall I ever understand this world?" he asked. "There is nothing on which it is so hard as poverty, and there is nothing it professes to condemn with such severity as the pursuit of wealth!"

"You fear the world too much, Ebenezer," said Isabel gently. "All your other hopes, that I loved so much, have merged into the hope of being beyond the world's sordid reproach. I have seen your nobler dreams die off, one by one, until only the desire for gain is left."

"I am not changed towards you. . . . Am I?"

"Yes, Ebenezer. You are. Your promise to me was made when you were poor, and content to be so. You were someone else then."

"I was a boy."

"Your own feeling tells you that you are not what you were. I am. The promise of happiness when we were one in heart is misery now that we are two. I see that only too clearly, and so I can release you." She looked sadly at the ring, then offered it to Ebenezer.

He did not take it. "Have I ever asked to be released?" he demanded.

"In words, no. But in a changed nature, yes. In everything that made my love of value to you, yes."

"No! That's not true!" interjected the older Scrooge.

"If you met me today, you would not love me," Isabel went on.

"I would! I do!" exclaimed Scrooge. "I still do. . . ." he added sadly.

"Ssssh!" hissed the ghost. "I'm trying to listen!"

Ebenezer remained silent.

Scrooge was deeply moved. The ghost put a restraining arm on him.

Isabel touched the pair of scales on the desk, placing the little ring on one side and a pile of gold coins on the other. The scales moved accordingly.

"Isabel, I find it impossible to discuss personal affairs during business hours. Now please," protested Ebenezer stuffily.

"You see?" said Isabel. "If you weigh me by gain, I weigh very little. And so I am not enough for you, and I release you—with a full heart, for the love of him you once were."

Scrooge smashed his fist silently on the desk, crying, *"No!* I love you, Isabel!"

Ebenezer went to speak, but Isabel turned away, not realizing.

Scrooge punched Ebenezer in the arm. "Say something, you fool! Tell her!"

Ebenezer struggled to say something.

"You may—the memory of what is past half makes me hope you will—have pain in this," continued Isabel. "But it will pass, and you will dismiss the recollection of it gladly, as an unprofitable dream, from which it happened well that you awoke."

Ebenezer shook his head.

Isabel kissed his cheek. "Be happy in the life you have chosen." She walked to the door.

"Isabel, wait! Come back!" cried Scrooge and Ebenezer together.

But she had gone.

Scrooge said brokenly to Ebenezer, "You *fool!"* and then to himself, "You fool!"

A single tear ran down Scrooge's otherwise expressionless face. He noticed the ring on the scale and regarded it with a sad smile.

Ebenezer suddenly ran out of the door to the head of the stairs and looked down. Then he came back into the room, and the old and the young Scrooge stood together at the window, watching their lost love walking away, out of their life.

Then Ebenezer returned to his desk and his neglected work. He took the coins from the scale, so that the little ring weighed down the other side. He picked it up and looked at it sadly. The scales balanced.

"Poor girl! I ruined her life!" said Scrooge.

"The only life you ruined was your own!" replied the ghost. "You did *her* a favour! Look!" She pointed in another direction.

Scrooge turned away. "No! I have seen enough!" he groaned.

The ghost gripped his arm, repeating, "Look!"

Scrooge looked.

Scrooge and the ghost stood looking at Isabel as she sat embroidering a tapestry in a fireside chair in her elegant living-room. She was as young and as beautiful as ever.

Scrooge sighed and shook his head. "She is so beautiful! But when is this?"

"Today," replied the ghost.

"It's not possible! She hasn't changed at all in twenty years!"

"Ah, but she has," said the ghost.

At that moment, Isabel, twenty years older but still very beautiful, entered the room and joined the daughter who was the image of herself as a girl.

"Her daughter!" exclaimed Scrooge in awe.

"Emma, fetch the children!" cried Isabel gaily. "Father and Grandpa are here with the presents. I heard the coach in the driveway."

Emma smiled her delight and hurried from the room.

As she did so, Isabel turned to greet her husband, who staggered into the room, calling for help, and completely hidden behind a mountain of gaily wrapped christmas boxes. Laughing, Isabel guided her husband as he tottered forward in the general direction of the magnificent Christmas tree that dominated the room, calling out as he did so, "This way, father. Follow me!"

Behind him came another similarly laden figure—Fezziwig—who exclaimed, laughing, "I would if I could see you, my boy!"

"Careful, father," said Isabel, lending a guiding hand to him, too.

Emma burst into the room with nine other children, all younger than herself. Shouts and screams of delight filled the air, and with ecstatic cries of "Daddy!" they hurled themselves at their unsuspecting father. The youngest child, a four-year-old boy, led the charge and promptly tripped and fell right under his father's feet.

"John, look out!" cried Isabel. But too late. Her husband stumbled over the little boy and, with a wild cry of despair, plunged headlong to the floor, showering the mountain of Christmas presents in every direction. Isabel, trying to save him, fell with him, and all the other children except Emma ended up on the floor in a great heap, with Fezziwig sprawling on top of everyone and sending another deluge of presents over them.

Helpless with laughter, and covered in boxes, ribbons, and wrapping papers, the entire family, spread out on the floor in front of the Christmas tree, presented as complete a picture of a Merry Christmas as anyone could imagine.

Only Emma remained standing—and as a spectator of this splendid mishap, her amusement was probably greater than anyone else's. She clapped her hands and threw her head back with redoubled mirth.

As Scrooge watched this scene of complete family happiness, a smile of great sadness came to his face. He watched the unbounded merriment of the moment—and especially the happy laughter of Isabel and young Emma—and remembered his long-forgotten happiness with Isabel, as he sang:

You—you were new to me.
You—you were spring.
You—you were true to me.
You—you were everything.

You—you were good for me.
You were my day.
Did all you could for me.
I let you go away.

And now I can see,
Now you're a dream gone by.
Oh, how could there be
Such a fool as I?

I, who must travel on,
What hope for me?
Dream where my past has gone.
Live with a memory—
You—my only hope.
You—my only love.
You . . . you . . . you . . .

As he sang, Scrooge thought about the things that might have been, realizing only too clearly what he had missed—not only the love of the woman he had lost, but also the renewed love that a daughter might have brought into his life. He closed his eyes, deeply moved, and his voice was soft and near the breaking as he begged, "Spirit, remove me from this place. I can bear no more."

"I'll take you home, Ebby," said the ghost reassuringly.

CHAPTER 4.—THE GHOST OF CHRISTMAS PRESENT

Slowly Scrooge opened his eyes. Then he realized that he was lying in bed, exactly as he had been doing when the church clock struck one and woke him up. The curtains round the bed were drawn. The Ghost of Christmas Past had vanished. Scrooge's face at first registered fear, then relief, then thoughtfulness. He frowned. "It was a dream! A nightmare!" he said at last. "First Marley, then the spirit . . . it was all in my imagination! It must have been! Stupid old fool—I got myself all upset over nothing!" His face permitted itself a thin smile.

The church clock struck two.

Scrooge almost jumped out of his skin at the first sound of the bell. A strange glow of light was seeping into the darkened room.

"I believe in you, spirit! Whoever you are! Have mercy on me!" cried Scrooge in terror.

He sat frozen with fear until the clock was totally silent, then he said slowly, "Two! The first at one, the second at two!"

He got up on his hands and knees on the bed and licked his dry lips in trepidation. He looked quickly from one side to the other, as though trying to anticipate some imminent disaster. "All right, whatever you are—I'm ready for you!"

Teeth and fists clenched, he steeled himself. Nothing happened. The silence was overwhelming. Scrooge began to tremble. "Nothing . . . perhaps it *was* a dream after all. . . . But this strange light is not nothing! Perhaps I am dreaming *now!*"

He pinched his arm. "Ouch! . . . No, it's not a dream. . . . There is something in the room!"

He poked his head through the bed-curtains and peeped out suspiciously into the room. All was still and silent, but the glow of light was stronger.

Scrooge got out of bed and looked nervously round. He began to walk slowly across the room. Then he halted abruptly, and his eyes widened as they spotted something.

The weird light was coming from his sitting-room, through the door. Rooted to the spot, Scrooge gazed at the light, uncertain whether or not to approach it. Finally he tiptoed to the door and listened—still no sound.

He stretched his hand slowly towards the doorknob, hesitated, then grasped it. The moment he did so, a deep, disembodied voice boomed eerily through the house. "Scrooge!" called the voice.

Scrooge bolted back across the room and leapt back into bed, nightcap

askew, his hand on his palpitating heart.

"Come here, Scrooge. I'm waiting for you."

Scrooge made no movement, except for an uncontrollable fit of shaking

"Or shall I come in there to get you?"

Scrooge was out of bed like a shot, making his way to the door, whimpering with fright. "I'm coming! I'm coming!"

He paused again at the door, gulped heavily, turned the doorknob, and went in.

Inside the sitting-room the brightness of the light shining in Scrooge's face dazzled him. He shaded his eyes with his hand.

"Is it too bright?" asked the voice.

Scrooge nodded and the light softened. Now he could see—and what a sight! His dreary sitting-room had been transformed into a scene of bountiful plenty, filled with a profusion of Christmas fare. There was every kind of fruit—apples and oranges and bananas and peaches and pineapples and grapes and coconuts. Holly, mistletoe, and ivy were everywhere, and heaped upon the floor were turkeys, geese, game, poultry, great joints of meat, sucking-pigs, mince-pies, plum-puddings, barrels of oysters, red-hot chestnuts, immense twelfth-cakes, and seething bowls of punch that filled the room with steam.

Enthroned amidst this glorious cornucopia sat a superb and jolly giant, wearing a magnificent deep-green velvet robe bordered with black fur, and on his head a holly wreath set with icicles that sparkled like enormous diamonds. Scrooge gazed up at him, stupefied. Either the room had got bigger or Scrooge had got smaller, for he was considerably less than waist-high to the giant.

The giant appeared extremely friendly, and his genial face creased into an expansive grin. "Welcome!" he boomed. "I am the Spirit of Christmas Present! Have a glass of punch!" He lifted a ladle from one of the steaming punch bowls, and poured a generous amount into a large golden goblet, which he thrust into Scrooge's hands, commanding him to drink.

Scrooge drank, a deep draught, as much from fear as from thirst. When his face emerged from the huge goblet, the marvellous nature of the brew he had been drinking was reflected in his ecstatic expression. "What *is* this drink?" he asked eagerly.

The giant chuckled. "Oh, just an inexpensive little nectar. A present from Bacchus himself, as a matter of fact. Mind you, he knows where to find these things!" He roared with laughter. Scrooge drank again.

"Now, look upon me!" commanded the giant.

Scrooge emerged again from the goblet and looked upon him, grinning. "You have never seen the like of me before!" continued the giant.

"Indeed no, sir!" answered Scrooge. "You are—er—uncommonly tall! And I would remember!" At this, they both roared with laughter.

Then the giant was suddenly serious. "You see," he said. "One sip of the spirit of Christmas, you contemptible wretch, and you are already a different man!"

He took the goblet away from Scrooge. Scrooge cowered back as the giant, angry now, but gentle in his anger, leaned forward in his throne, towering over Scrooge's head, and looked down at him. "And yet how many of my brothers, who each year bring the spirit of goodwill to earth, have you rejected in your miserable lifetime?" he demanded.

"I have never met your brothers, sir."

"You have never looked for them!"

"How many of them *are* there?"

"What year is this?"

"Eighteen hundred and sixty."

"Then I have eighteen hundred and fifty-nine brothers!" said the giant. "Each year at this time, one of us visits this puny planet to spread some happiness and good cheer, and to remove as many as we can of the causes of human misery!" He leaned closer to Scrooge, his voice a menacing rumble. "Which is why I have come to see *you*, Ebenezer Scrooge!"

Scrooge was petrified. The giant picked him up with one hand, stood him on the table, and looked at him closely. Scrooge peered down towards the floor and reeled dizzily.

The giant chuckled. "You're a funny-looking creature!" he exclaimed. "I found it hard to believe that you would be as horrible as my brothers described you, but now that I look at you, I'm not at all sure they weren't understating the truth!"

"Let me assure you, sir," said Scrooge with dignity, "that you are looking at a man of the highest principles and the most generous spirit!" He hiccuped, and the pompom of his nightcap fell over one eye.

The giant rocked with laughter. Scrooge flung both arms around a statue of a woodland nymph and clung on for dear life to stop himself from falling.

The giant peered at him closely again. "Generous spirit?" he echoed. "You don't know the meaning of the phrase, you pitiful Scrooge—but you are about to find out! Here, try a drop of this!" As he spoke, he poured some white fluid into a sparkling crystal chalice, and handed it to Scrooge, who asked suspiciously what it was. On being urged to taste it, Scrooge sniffed cautiously at the drink, then sipped it. He paused, then drained the chalice dry.

The giant nodded and smiled. "Do you like it?" he inquired.

"It's wonderful!" exclaimed Scrooge. "I've never tasted anything like it!"

"Of course you haven't!"

"What is it?" asked Scrooge again, this time eagerly.

"The milk of human kindness. There are more good things in life, Scrooge, than you can possibly imagine!"

"I'm sure there are!" replied Scrooge. "Can I have some more?"

The giant's eyes twinkled as he refilled Scrooge's proffered chalice. And then he burst into song:

> *Ebenezer Scrooge,*
> *The sins of man are huge.*
> *A never-ending symphony*
> *Of villainy and infamy,*
> *Duplicity, deceit and subterfuge.*
> *And no one's worse than*
> *Ebenezer Scrooge.*
>
> *Though man's a handy candidate for Hell,*
> *I must admit*
> *Life sometimes has*
> *Its brighter side as well!*
>
> *I like life! Life likes me!*
> *Life and I fairly fully agree—*
> *Life is fine! Life is good!*
> *'Specially mine,*
> *Which is just as it should be!*
>
> *I like pouring the wine,*
> *And why not?*
> *Life's a pleasure*
> *That I deny not!*

I like life! Here and now!
Life and I made a mutual vow!
Till I die,
Life and I
We'll both try to be better somehow!

And if life were a woman,
She would be my wife!
Why?
Because I
Like life!

When the giant had finished his song, Scrooge exclaimed crossly, "That's all very well for you! I hate life." He was suddenly morose and depressed.

The giant roared with laughter and poured out another huge goblet of the milk of human kindness. "Nonsense, man!" he cried heartily. Then he sang, *"Why?"*

"Because life hates me!" sang Scrooge in reply. "That's why!" He jumped down off the table, quite drunk.

"Scrooge, you're an even bigger fool than I took you for! I've never heard such a lot of self-pitying drivel. You don't even know *how* to live! Now listen to me." Then the giant burst into song again: *"I like life . . ."* He urged Scrooge to continue.

Reluctantly, at first, Scrooge shook off his gloom as the giant lavished food and drink on him, and he finally joined in the song. Their singing grew more and more boisterous until at last, in the very best of drunken high spirits, they flew out through the window and floated across the night sky, tra-la-la-ing at the tops of their voices.

Suddenly, the giant dived down towards the earth, holding his companion firmly by the arm. Scrooge whooped for joy as they dropped out of the sky into a large snowdrift piled up across the street from Bob Cratchit's house. The giant lay back with a contented sigh.

Scrooge had come down to earth in every sense and was once again his old crusty self. He shook himself out of his daze and glared at the giant, complaining testily, "You're blocking the street."

The giant replied that there was no traffic.

"I'd like to know what the devil I'm doing rolling around on my back in a pile of snow in the middle of a freezing cold winter's night—that's what

I'd like to know!" grumbled Scrooge. "Anyway, where are we?"

The giant pointed to the wretched little house across the street. "That," he said, "is the lavish home of Robert Cratchit, Esquire, who owes both the opulence of his surroundings and the magnificence of his Christmas celebrations to the high principles and generous spirit of his employer!" Mockingly, he repeated Scrooge's own description of himself.

That brought Scrooge down to earth with an even bigger bump. He turned away to hide the look of guilt which flooded over his face. Then he said, "I want to look in the window."

"It will cost you nothing, which I'm sure will be good news for you!" said the giant satirically.

"Will they be able to see me?" asked Scrooge.

"No," said the giant, "which I'm sure will be good news for them!"

"I could do with another of those drinks," hinted Scrooge.

"Later," said the giant firmly. "For the time being it's better that you see things as they really are!"

Scrooge walked over to the house. He rubbed a porthole in the frost on the window-pane and peered through it.

Inside the shabby parlour, various members of the Cratchit family were busily engaged in making their paltry Christmas provisions look like the Lord Mayor's banquet. They were all in great good spirits.

Mrs. Cratchit, Bob's plump and pretty wife, lifted the lid of the copper and fished out a rather undernourished, muslin-wrapped plum-pudding with her copper-stick, sniffed it approvingly, and lowered it with loving care back into the bubbling cauldron.

At the stove, Bob Cratchit stirred a small saucepan containing his home-made punch, and with great ceremony lifted the wooden spoon to his lips to sample the mixture. "Nectar! Pure nectar!" he cried, closing his eyes in rapture. "And at threepence a pint, you can't really grumble!" He offered his wife a sip of punch.

"Bob Cratchit, you're a genius!" she cried approvingly, prompting an exclamation of "Silly woman!" from Scrooge at the window.

Bob grinned at his wife. "What a tragedy that Her Majesty and His Worship the Lord Mayor couldn't be with us tonight, my dear!" he said. "They don't know what they're missing!" At his words, gales of happy laughter swept through the parlour.

At the table, two smaller girl Cratchits were kneading a large mound of stuffing. One of them informed her father that the stuffing was ready. Bob promptly set down his wooden spoon and with immense pride carried to the table a crockery platter on which sat a scrawny, poorly plucked goose, observing as he did so, "The marriage of roast goose and sage and onion stuffing à la Cratchit is one of the culinary miracles of our day—a living legend throughout the length and breadth of Camden Town!"

He set the platter down upon the table. The pile of stuffing was bigger than the goose, and Bob looked at it doubtfully. "The only remaining problem, my dears, is whether to put the stuffing inside the goose or the goose inside the stuffing!" This was greeted with renewed gusts of mirth from the family. "But since the ultimate intention is to put them both inside ourselves," he went on, "I don't suppose it much matters!"

Scrooge watched as Tiny Tim and Kathy burst into the parlour, looking highly delighted with life.

Bob Cratchit left what he was doing, picked up his son and kissed him, and hugged Kathy, exclaiming, "And here they are—the one and only carol-singing Cratchits, newly returned from their triumphant musical tour of Regent's Park and the Euston Road."

The family cheered and applauded the heroes' return, and Mrs. Cratchit asked, "How did you do, Tiny Tim?"

"Tenpence ha'penny!" cried Tiny Tim exultantly, causing redoubled cheers as he proudly displayed his handful of copper coins.

"Tenpence ha'penny!" echoed his father. "Another fantastic coup by young Timothy Cratchit, the financial wizard! At only seven years of age, the youngest millionaire in the vast Cratchit empire!"

Bob set Tiny Tim on a chair at the parlour table and returned to his simmering saucepan of punch. He took it and a tray of half-a-dozen minute glasses across to the table. He poured punch and distributed the glasses to his family, saying as he did so, "Ladies and gentlemen, if I may steal a moment of your valuable time, I would ask you to drink to the sparkling good health of the two gentlemen whose industry and generosity have made possible our sumptuous Christmas repast—Master Timothy Cratchit—and Mr. Ebenezer Scrooge!"

At the window, Scrooge was surprised and pleased to hear his name mentioned in this context—until he saw the reaction of the other members of the Cratchit family. The smiles faded from the children's faces, and Mrs. Cratchit looked at her husband as though he were mad. "Mr. Scrooge?" she cried. "What are you trying to do—spoil our Christmas?"

"His money paid for the goose, my dear," returned Bob mildly.

"No! *Your* money paid for the goose!"

"But *he* paid me the money!" insisted Bob.

"Because *you* earned it, my love! Believe me! Fifteen shillings a week at threepence an hour, and not a penny raise in eight years! You earned it!"

"Mr. Scrooge assures me that times are hard."

"He's right! For you, they are! But not for himself!"

"Nonetheless, my dear," insisted Bob mildly, "he is the Founder of our Feast, and we shall drink to him!"

Scrooge nodded in agreement, and beckoned over his shoulder for the giant to come and watch with him.

"The Founder of our Feast, indeed!" cried Mrs. Cratchit. "I wish I had him here! I'd give him a piece of my mind to feast upon, and he'd have indigestion for a month!"

"Ethel, my dear, the children!" protested Bob gently. "Christmas Day!"

At the window, the giant rubbed a second and larger porthole on the frosted pane, and his face appeared in it, alongside Scrooge's face.

Mrs. Cratchit exclaimed, "It needs to be Christmas Day, Bob, to drink to the health of such an odious, stingy, hard, unfeeling, and altogether rotten man as Mr. Ebenezer Scrooge!"

Scrooge gave the giant an embarrassed smile. The giant chuckled.

"But—," objected Bob.

"You know he is, Bob," said his wife. "Nobody knows it better than you, my poor love."

The sparkle seemed to have left Bob Cratchit. He touched his wife's hand, smiled at her sadly, and raised his glass to her. "Christmas Day, my dear."

"Children," said Mrs. Cratchit, "we shall drink to your father, for all the love and happiness he gives us, and to Tiny Tim, for the health we wish him. . . ." She caught Bob's eye looking up at her, smiled, and put her arm round his shoulders as she stood beside his chair. "And, for the sake of your father and of Christmas Day, but not for his own sake, I'll even drink to that old miser, Mr. Scrooge. Long life to him, and to us all!"

"A Merry Christmas to us all, my dears," said Bob. "God bless us!"

"God bless us, every one," added Tiny Tim.

They drank, and Bob squeezed Tiny Tim's hand. Then he cried, "As I said to the Lord Mayor, if Her Most Gracious Majesty gets bored, I said, you just wheel her over 'ere to Camden Town, I said! A glass of Bob Cratchit's hot punch, and a song from young Tiny Tim, and we'll have her back on her regal feet in no time!"

Everyone laughed and shouted "Hear, hear!" as they raised their recharged glasses.

"There's the punch!" cried Bob. "Now where's our song, my Tiny Tim?"

All heads turned to Tiny Tim, who blushed, but finally responded to the vociferous urging of his brothers and sisters. Bob lifted him up to stand on his chair, and introduced him to the family in dumb show with a flourish and a low bow, and the family cheered and applauded. Then they all fell silent, and Tiny Tim started to sing. He had a voice of pure gold:

On a beautiful day
That I dream about
In a world I would love to see

Is a beautiful place
Where the sun comes out
And it shines in the sky for me.

On this beautiful winter's morning
If my wish could come true
Somehow,

Then the beautiful day
That I dream about
Would be here
And now.

Outside the window, the giant, who had crouched down on his hands and knees to see into the parlour window, scrambled to his feet. He noticed Scrooge wiping a tear from the corner of his eye as he turned away from the window, and smiled to himself, remarking, "What an unpleasant child! You know, there are few things more nauseating to see than a happy family enjoying themselves at Christmas! Do you not agree?"

"I think Bob Cratchit's really rather fond of me!" said Scrooge.

The giant roared with laughter. "And so's his wife! Couldn't you tell?" He wiped the snow from his shoulders and it cascaded down upon Scrooge's head like a miniature blizzard.

"Mind you," continued Scrooge, "she doesn't really know me!"

"That is one of the few things wherein Fate has blessed her!"

"And Tiny Tim," asked Scrooge suddenly, "what will become of him?"

"What's this?" asked the giant in surprise. "Concern over a sick child? Have you taken leave of your senses?"

"Don't mock me, spirit," said Scrooge. "Is the child *very* sick?—not that it's of any great importance to me whether he is or not, of course . . . but is he?" There was a pause, and the giant remained silent. "You mean, he's seriously ill?" Still the giant said nothing. "Will he . . . live?" Scrooge hesitated a little over the last word. There was another pause, during which the giant stared impassively at Scrooge. Scrooge grew angry. "Well, *will* he?" he demanded impatiently.

"What does it matter to you, Ebenezer Scrooge? If he is going to die, then he had better do it, and decrease the surplus population!"

Scrooge hung his head to hear his own words quoted by the spirit.

"Come, we must be on our way!" said the giant. "My time is short."

They stopped outside an elegant row of terraced houses in Bloomsbury.
"We shall pay one more call," said the giant.
"No . . . no more. . . ." pleaded Scrooge.
"On your nephew," continued the giant.
"No!" cried Scrooge.
In the living-room of the house belonging to Scrooge's nephew, the nephew, his wife, and about a dozen friends were standing in front of the fireplace. Scrooge and the giant were sitting on a sofa at the far end of the room.

Scrooge's nephew raised his glass and said, "Ladies and gentlemen, will you please honour me with your undivided attention? That famous moment is arrived that I know you all look forward to in this house every Christmas Eve, when I ask you to drink to the good health and long life of my celebrated Uncle Ebenezer!"

As he listened to his nephew's speech, Scrooge's face lit up and he said, "Sounds to me as if he knows I'm here."

"Of course not. He can't see you," replied the giant.

"Hmm," said Scrooge. "Maybe I've misjudged him."

Meanwhile, the nephew's guests responded to the toast he proposed—albeit with no great show of enthusiasm—and drank Scrooge's health.

"Harry," said one of the guests, "I've visited you every Christmas for the past five years, and to this day I can never understand this extraordinary ritual of drinking to the health of your Uncle Ebenezer! Everybody knows he's the most miserable old skinflint that ever walked God's earth!"

Scrooge was very put out by this. "Who's he?" he asked the giant.

"Oh, just a friend."

"A friend?" echoed Scrooge.

"My dear Tom," his nephew was explaining, "it's very simple. He is indeed the most despicable old miser. . . ."

"What's this?" cried Scrooge.

"Worse than you could ever possibly imagine. . . ." went on his nephew. The giant chuckled.

Scrooge glared at him. "You find this amusing?" he asked sharply.

The giant nodded, still chuckling.

"May one ask why?" inquired Scrooge sarcastically.

"He likes you!"

"I can tell!" rejoined Scrooge ironically.

"But I look at it this way—," his nephew was saying. "If I can wish a Merry Christmas to him, who is beyond dispute the most obnoxious and parsimonious of all living creatures . . ."

"Hear, hear!" cried his guests.

"The scoundrel!" burst out Scrooge, filled with righteous indignation. "The villain! If he were in my will, I'd disinherit him!"

The giant was practically helpless with laughter by this time.

" . . . then I know in my heart I am truly a man of goodwill!" Scrooge's nephew concluded humorously.

"Now that I *will* drink to!" cried his friend. All the guests joined in the toast.

Scrooge was beside himself. "Spirit, is there no end to my humiliation?" he demanded.

"Wait," replied the spirit, "there is more to come!"

"I'm sure there is!" Scrooge waited, cowed, for the next blow to fall.

"Besides," added the nephew, "I like old Scrooge!"

Scrooge perked up at this.

"What did I tell you?" asked the giant.

"You're joking!" cried the nephew's friend.

"I truly do!" cried the nephew. "God knows, I have little enough reason to do so after the way he treated my mother, his sister, but I can't help feeling that hidden somewhere inside that loathsome old carcass of his . . ."

"Loathsome old carcass?!" echoed Scrooge.

" . . . there is a different man fighting to get out!" finished the nephew.

"Careful, Harry—," warned his friend, "he may be even worse than the one you know!"

There was laughter from everyone except Scrooge.

"God forbid!" cried the nephew. "Anyway, that's why I invite him to come here every Christmas, and will continue to do so, in the forlorn hope that one day he might just drop by and pick up enough goodwill to raise his clerk's wages by five shillings a week! God knows, it's high time he did!"

"Hear, hear! Bravo!" cried the guests.

Scrooge's face darkened at once when he heard this. "He's very free with other people's money, this fellow!" he exclaimed indignantly. "I never heard of such a thing!"

An extremely pretty girl, obviously the nephew's wife, broke up the discussion, saying firmly to her husband, "All right, Harry, now that's enough. I refuse to have my Christmas haunted by Uncle Ebenezer!"

Scrooge found this amusing. "If only you knew, my dear!" he said. Then he walked over to her, shrieked a mock ghostly shriek, and pulled a face at her. The giant roared with laughter.

"We'll have some music and then we'll play some splendid party games," cried the nephew's wife. "There's a charming new game called The Minister's Cat! It's very funny, and you all end up getting angry when you lose!"

A servant appeared with a tray of drinks. The guests helped themselves. So did Scrooge, but because he was a spirit his hand passed right through the glass and the drink. The giant promptly produced a flask and two glasses, apparently out of nowhere, and poured them a drink.

"What's this?" asked Scrooge suspiciously.

"Something better than they're having!" came the reply. That was good enough for Scrooge. He tasted the drink. It was good, and he brightened up immediately. The music struck up, and people started dancing. Scrooge drained the glass, handed it to the giant, and in the best of spirits started to clap his hands in time to the music. The tune was "December the Twenty-Fifth," which he remembered from his days at Fezziwig's. The giant nodded approvingly.

Afterwards, they grouped themselves round the fire to play a fast-moving party game in which each of them in turn had to think of a different adjective beginning with the same letter, in time to the clapping of their hands. Anyone who broke the tempo was "out."

Although nobody could see or hear him, Scrooge was very much involved in the game, prompting everyone in turn and thoroughly enjoying himself. All the guests were engrossed in the game, and there was great tension and concentration. Round the circle they said in turn:

"The minister's cat is a marvellous cat."

"The minister's cat is a marmalade cat."

"The minister's cat is a miserable cat."

"The minister's cat is a merciful cat."

"The minister's cat is a m-m-m . . er . . ." stammered the nephew when it came to his turn.

"Merry! Merry! Say merry!" prompted Scrooge eagerly.

"Too late! You're out!" cried the nephew's wife.

"Oh, bother it!" he exclaimed. Everybody laughed and the clapping petered out.

"I told you to say merry!" scolded Scrooge. "What's the matter with you? Are you stupid?" He appealed to the giant. "He's always been stupid!"

"Right, what's next?" asked the nephew's wife.

"N," said Scrooge.

"N," said the guest whose turn came next.

"Right, N," cried the nephew's wife. "Begin!"

They all started to clap again in unison and continued round the circle:

"The minister's cat is a naughty cat."

"The minister's cat is a nasty cat."

"The minister's cat is a n-n . . ." He was slightly hesitant.

Scrooge, prompting, yelled in his ear with fervent intensity, "Nice!"

"N-nice cat."

Scrooge collapsed with relief, and the game continued. The giant was smiling.

Later on that evening, the giant had fallen asleep. The guests were departing, and Scrooge was with the guests lining up to say good night to the host and hostess. He took the outstretched hand of his nephew vacated by the previous guest, but it fell through his own, which did not exist. "Thank you, my boy," said Scrooge warmly. "What a wonderful evening. The Minister's Cat game—splendid—I thought I was rather good at it! Good night . . . good night . . . thank you. I can honestly say I haven't enjoyed a Christmas as much as this since I was a young apprentice at old Fezziwig's—oh, so many years ago. . . . What Christmases we used to have in those days. Fantastic, they were. . . . He had this daughter . . . reminded me a little bit of your mother she did. . . ." But his nephew could not see him, and he continued to chat to his guests, promising to get his uncle there for them next year.

The giant woke up with a start, glanced at the time on the grandfather clock, and leapt to his feet. Scrooge went on reminiscing, lost in memories.

He was still talking when they reached the alleyway outside his lodgings, where the solitary gaslamp shed its dim light. Scrooge did not yet realize where he was, for his thoughts were far away from the present time and place. His eyes filled with tears as he continued, ". . . Her name was Isabel . . . oh, Isabel. . . ."

Nostalgically he sang:

. . . They say happiness is the folly of fools.
Pity poor me. One of the fools.
Happiness was standing beside me.
I could see her. She could see me.
Happiness is whatever you want it to be. . . .

Scrooge's voice trailed away and his gaze travelled slowly upwards. "Where are we?" he demanded.

"I've brought you home, Scrooge," replied the giant.

Scrooge looked around him vaguely. "Oh, yes . . . home. You're not going, are you?"

"My time upon this little planet is very brief," said the giant. "It ends tonight."

"So soon?" asked Scrooge. "But we still have so much to talk about! . . . Haven't we?"

"There is never enough time to say or do all the things we would wish. The thing is to do as much as you can in the time you have," said the giant. "I must go. Remember, Scrooge, time is short, and suddenly you're not there any more. . . ." Even as he spoke, he disappeared, his voice and his form fading simultaneously.

Scrooge shivered and looked about him in the gloom. "No, wait! Come back!" he cried. "Where are you? Why is it so dark?"

He realized where he was—back in his bed. The room seemed darker than before. "Oh, my God! Look where I am! What am I doing here?!!" he cried, close to panic.

Then he calmed down and tried to get control of himself. "I'm in bed," he muttered, "that's what I'm doing here! This is where I'm supposed to be in the middle of the night!" He held his head between his hands, forcing himself to concentrate. "Was I dreaming again?" he asked. "I must have been! That giant—I must be mad—there are no giants!—there are no ghosts!"

Far away he heard the giant's laughter echoing eerily through the night, and the clanking of Marley's chain. He shuddered convulsively, but fought to control his voice and his emotions. "There *are* ghosts! Yes there are! And giants! And I believe in them! I do!" he babbled. "Oh, my God! What a nightmare!" And he buried his face in his hands.

CHAPTER 5.—THE GHOST OF CHRISTMAS YET TO COME

The church clock began to strike. It was three o'clock.

Scrooge looked up, startled, and his mouth dropped open. "Three already?" he exclaimed. "It can't be!"

Then he gasped with fear as a black shadow fell across his face. "Oh, no! Not again!" He looked up, dreading what he was about to see.

Looming over him at the bedside was a shapeless black phantom—a fearsome sight.

Scrooge swallowed convulsively and closed his eyes, his nerves in shreds. In a hollow, broken voice he said, "I t-t-take it, sir, from your somewhat unconventional apparel, that you are the Ghost of Christmas Yet To Come."

The phantom nodded.

"And you-you-you are about to take me on a t-tour of things that have not yet happened, but which will happen in the time before us. Is that not so, spirit?" Still trembling, he opened his eyes.

Again the phantom nodded.

"I thought so. . . . Oh, God! . . . I don't suppose by any chance you happen to have about your—er—person a small flask of that splendid libation which your—er—predecessor—the tall one—he used to carry—er—no, I don't suppose you would. . . ."

The phantom was immobile.

Scrooge closed his eyes again, and seemed to be trying to summon up all his reserves of inner strength. "Ghost of the Future!" he said at length, "I fear you more than any apparition I have ever seen. But as I know your purpose is to do me good, and as I hope to live to be another man from what I was, I am prepared to bear you company, and do it with a thankful heart. Will you speak to me?"

Still the phantom gave him no reply, but lifted one of its shrouded arms and pointed towards the window and out into the night.

Scrooge nodded timidly and scrambled off the end of the bed, his nightcap awry. "Very well," he said. "Lead on, spirit! The night is waning fast, and I know it is precious time to me. Lead on!"

The phantom raised both arms skywards. The windows flew open and an icy gale blew through the room. Thunder and lightening filled the dark sky. Scrooge stood shivering in his long nightshirt, his teeth chattering with cold. The force of the wind increased until it was like a typhoon. With a wild cry of fear, Scrooge was swept off his feet, and he and the phantom went swirling out of the window into the night.

A young man was giving a final polish to the brass name-plaque outside Scrooge's office. He finished with a flourish and then stepped back and bowed to a large crowd gathered round the doorway. Cheers and applause greeted his gesture. Once again it was Christmastime.

Scrooge and the phantom stood at the edge of the crowd. "I know that fellow!" cried Scrooge. "It's Tom Jenkins, the hot soup man. Owes me six pounds! I must say he looks uncommonly happy for a man so deep in debt."

And indeed, Tom Jenkins was grinning from ear to ear as he addressed the crowd. "Ladies and gentlemen," he said, "we are gathered 'ere today because we are united by a common bond—namely, our feelings of gratitude to Mr. Ebenezer Scrooge!"

The crowd roared its raucous agreement.

Scrooge could hardly believe his ears. "This is the future?" he asked the phantom incredulously.

The phantom nodded.

It was clear that Scrooge, already in a highly emotional condition, was deeply touched. "I had no idea!" he exclaimed.

Tom Jenkins was saying, "I don't think any one of us could ever 'ope to find the words to describe the true depth of that feeling. . . ."

Again the crowd demonstrated its mood with a roar of approval and laughter.

In the crowd Scrooge saw the smiling faces of the people he had visited on Christmas Eve, including the Punch and Judy man and the two old ladies who ran the children's clothing stall in the market. "These people! I know them all!" cried Scrooge. "They are all my debtors!"

The phantom nodded.

"And they are paying tribute to me! They love me! I never knew!"

"All right, my friends. Please try to control your emotions!" continued Tom Jenkins, trying to quieten the mob. "I just want to say, on be'alf of us all, that those of us what has been in debt to Mr. Scrooge these past months and years will never be able to repay the great and beautiful favour 'e's done for us all today!"

The crowd went wild with delight, with cheers and tears of laughter.

"What did I do? What did I do?" asked Scrooge excitedly. "Whatever it was, it has made them truly happy! And I am the cause!"

Overcome, he turned his back on the crowd to hide his emotion, and thus missed seeing the true cause of their ecstasy, which was indeed Ebenezer

Scrooge—in his coffin, being carried out of the office by four grim-faced, top-hatted undertakers and borne away down the street on a cart. The crowd cheered the coffin on its way with a happy, impromptu chorus of "For He's A Jolly Good Fellow" in time to the marching feet of the pall-bearers.

As the cortege disappeared from view, Scrooge turned back to face the crowd and threw his arms up in the air, crying, "My friends! I thank you from the bottom of my heart! I shall remember this moment until my dying day! And may I say with all humility that I have laboured unceasingly all my life to be worthy of this moving demonstration of your feelings towards me!" He was unaware of the irony of his words!

Behind him, Tom Jenkins brandished Scrooge's infamous black book, and as Scrooge addressed the crowd, Tom proceeded to rip out the pages and toss them into the air. As the pages fluttered down, the crowd cheered wildly, and the unsuspecting Scrooge thought happily that they were cheering his speech.

The fact that no one could hear a word he said—or was even aware that he was there!—could not detract from the passionate sincerity of Scrooge's speech. Nor could anything detract from the equally passionate happiness of the crowd. Led by Tom Jenkins, who was sitting astride the coffin, they set off down the street, singing and dancing, to celebrate the great liberation which Scrooge's death had given them. Scrooge, every bit as jubilant as they were, joined in:

> *On behalf of all the people*
> *Who have assembled here*
> *I would merely like to mention, if I may,*
> *That our unanimous attitude*
> *Is one of lasting gratitude*
> *For what our friend*
> *Has done for us today!*
> *And therefore I would simply like to say . . .*
>
> *Thank you very much!*
> *Thank you very much!*
> *That's the nicest thing*
> *That anyone's ever done for me!*
> *It may sound Double Dutch,*
>
> *But my delight is such*
> *I feel as if a losing war's*
> *Been won for me!*
>
> *And if I had a flag*
> *I'd hang my flag out—*
> *To add a sort of final victory touch!*
> *But since I left my flag at home*
> *I'll simply have to say*
> *Thank you very, very, very much!*

Thank you very much!
Thank you very much!
That's the nicest thing
That anyone's ever done for me!
The future looks all right!
In fact it looks so bright
I feel as if
They're polishing the sun for me!

And if I had a drum
I'd have to bang it!
To add a sort of rumpty tumpty touch!
But since I left my drummer at home
I'll simply have to say
Thank you very, very, very much!
Thank you very, very, very much!

It was a song of joyful celebration, and Scrooge's contribution to it was all the more disarming for his complete ignorance of the emotions that inspired it.

The motley parade of Scrooge's carousing debtors went past Bob Cratchit's house, still singing heartily.

Scrooge, bringing up the rear, recognized the house and stopped. The crowd and the sound of their singing slowly faded into the distance. The phantom pointed to the parlour window. Scrooge's mood changed into one of anxiety. He walked slowly to the window, rubbed a porthole in its frosted covering, and looked in.

Inside the parlour, Mrs. Cratchit and the four eldest children were seated around the table. The room was half-heartedly prepared for Christmas, and the sadness in the faces of the Cratchits was in depressing contrast to their happiness on Scrooge's previous visit. Mrs. Cratchit and her daughters were sewing, while Peter was reading a book.

Suddenly, Mrs. Cratchit laid her work down on the table and covered her eyes with her hand, saying, "The colour hurts my eyes, and I mustn't show weak eyes to your father when he gets home. It must be near his time."

Peter shut his book. "Past it," he said. "But I think he has walked a little slower these last few evenings."

They were all very quiet again. At last Mrs. Cratchit said in a steady, cheerful voice, that only faltered once, "I have known him walk with Tiny Tim upon his shoulder very fast indeed."

"So have I. Often," said Peter.

"So have I," added Joy.

"But he was light to carry and his father loved him. So it was no trouble—no trouble," said Mrs. Cratchit.

Scrooge gazed searchingly round the room, and finally he noticed something hanging from a hook on the wall between the stove and the parlour door. It was Tiny Tim's crutch.

Scrooge turned away from the window. Staring coldly at the phantom, he demanded, "Where is Tiny Tim? Take me wherever he is!"

The phantom took Scrooge to a small graveyard. He could hear the faint voice of Tiny Tim singing the song he had sung for his family the previous Christmas:

> *On this beautiful winter's morning,*
> *If my wish could come true*
> *Somehow,*
>
> *Then the beautiful day*
> *That I dream about*
> *Would be here*
> *And now.*

Bob Cratchit, sad-eyed but smiling, was kneeling in front of a little white wooden cross. Beyond the grey churchyard the church loomed black and sombre against a sky the colour of slate. And in that bleak and dismal scene the only touch of colour was provided by the bunch of violets in Bob's hand. Scrooge and the phantom stood behind him.

"It's going to be a lovely Christmas, my Tiny Tim—," Bob said, "maybe not as lovely as last year—the singing won't be as good, for one thing . . ." His voice faltered. " . . . but we'll do our best for you . . . we truly will . . . oh, Tim! My little fellow!" He almost broke down, but managed to keep a brave face in front of Tiny Tim. He attempted his usual cheery smile, which slipped a little.

A single tear ran down Scrooge's cheek, and he said, "Poor Tiny Tim!"

Bob placed the bunch of violets at the foot of the little cross, on which was inscribed: "Timothy Cratchit—1854–1861—Aged 7 years."

"Brought you a little present, Tim—those little flowers you always liked so much. . . ." said Bob. "I must go now. I promised your mother I'd be home in time to help her serve the Christmas dinner. We'll drink to you, my Tim . . . and I'll come and see you tomorrow . . . same time. . . ." He got to his feet and, with a last sad look at the pathetic little grave, he hurried away.

Scrooge watched him go. Then he said, "Spirit, you have shown me a Christmas yet to come which mingles great happiness with great sadness. But I want to know what will become of me still further into the future."

The phantom turned and pointed ahead of him.

Scrooge, his face alive with renewed excitement, turned to view this fresh prospect. His eyes filled with terror and a strangled cry escaped his lips. "No!"

At his feet lay a plain, drab, flat, grey slab of stone, and engraved upon it were the words EBENEZER SCROOGE.

Scrooge turned back in unspeakable horror to the phantom, who pointed from him to the grave and then advanced slowly towards him. Scrooge started to back away, mesmerized with fear. His voice was no more than a hoarse whisper as he said, "No . . . oh, no! Please . . . I beg you! I have seen the error of my ways! Truly I will repent." But it was too late.

Scrooge reached out to grasp the outstretched hand of the phantom, then he dropped it with a gasp. It was the hand of a skeleton. Scrooge looked up dizzily and saw the grotesque face of the skeleton grinning down at him. "Death! . . . You are Death!" he whispered. The skeleton's head swam before him as he lost consciousness and pitched forward into the tomb.

Scrooge was falling, falling—into a bottomless void that turned from blue to purple to red to pitch black. He fell as if in a dream—drifting almost gently downwards, and somehow detached from fear. He seemed to be falling through all eternity into total darkness.

In the echoing distance he heard the voice of Marley singing:

> *See the phantoms*
> *Filling the sky around you!*
> *They confound you,*
> *I can tell—*
> *These inhabitants of Hell!*

And then Scrooge himself joined in the mournful dirge:

Poor wretches
For whom the sun has ceased to shine.
My soul is filled with fear
Lest their fearful fate
Be mine!

The light grew brighter. Scrooge blinked. Then he blinked again. "I am dead. . . ." he thought. "I am a spirit . . . and when I move my arms and legs, there will be a mighty chain around them—just like Jacob Marley's! . . . only bigger!"

From a confusion of tormented sound, he distinguished the dragging of a heavy chain and the far-off voice of Jacob Marley calling his name: "Scroo-o-oge . . ."

Scrooge sat up hastily and saw the figure of Marley standing over him in the heavy red light. Scrooge looked at his legs. To his immense relief, there was no chain. He smiled. "No chain! Then I must be in Heaven!" he cried. "No, I can't be—Marley's here! . . . Marley? Where am I?"

"That is a somewhat superfluous question!" answered Marley drily. "I should have thought it was obvious!"

Scrooge looked around him gloomily. "Yes, I suppose so."

"Anyway," continued Marley, "I heard you were coming in today, so I thought I'd come and meet you and show you to your quarters. Nobody else wanted to."

"That's very civil of you, Marley. I—er—I *am* dead, aren't I?"

"Dead as a doornail! We've never had anybody here who wasn't!" replied Marley with a brief, morose chuckle.

"It's really a rather pleasant sensation!"

"Oh yes, you'll soon get used to it!"

"I had rather hoped I'd end up in Heaven!" confided Scrooge.

"Didn't we all? Anyway, you may take comfort from the fact that there are far more people down here than there are up there! In fact, overcrowding is one of our more serious problems! Which is why your office is so small!"

"Office?" echoed Scrooge.

"Your activities in life were so pleasing to Lucifer that he has appointed you to be his personal clerk—a singular honour!"

"But I . . . " stammered Scrooge.

"You will, so to speak, be to him what Bob Cratchit was to you!"

The blood drained from Scrooge's face and he got to his feet, appalled. "No! Oh, no! That's not fair! It's . . . it's . . ."

Marley permitted himself a mean smile. "It's diabolical!" he supplied. "Now you know why it's called Hell! I must confess I find it not altogether unamusing. One thing about Lucifer—he does have a sense of humour. It's a bit macabre, of course, but it's better than nothing! There's your office over there! Oh, and watch out for the rats—they tend to eat the ledgers!"

"Rats?" faltered Scrooge, aghast.

Marley pointed to a minute cell dimly visible behind them. He opened the door and Scrooge looked at its dank interior with horror and distaste. He could hear the rats squeaking and scuttling around inside. Then he poked his head in and shivered. "It's freezing cold in there!" he complained.

"Yes, he turned the heat off! He thought it might make you drowsy!" Marley smiled again. "You'll be the only man in Hell who's cold!" He sniggered to himself as he turned and walked away, dragging his heavy chain.

"Marley, come back!" cried Scrooge frantically. "Please don't leave me!"

Marley turned, his old morose self once more. "You know I cannot stay!" he grumbled. "I am doomed to eternal wandering with this intolerable burden!" He indicated his chain as he spoke.

Scrooge brightened perceptibly. "I suppose I should be grateful that I haven't got one of those!"

"Ah, I forgot to tell you! I knew there was something!" exclaimed Marley. "They apologize that your chain wasn't ready in time for your arrival, but it's so big they've had to take on extra devils at the foundry to finish it!"

Scrooge groaned.

Marley sniggered again and added, "It's even bigger than I thought it would be! Wait! Here it is now!"

Towards them came four shadowy figures bent double and groaning beneath the mighty weight of Scrooge's chain. By comparison with it, Marley's chain looked like a charm bracelet!

Horrified, Scrooge cringed back against his cell. "I can't wear that! I'll never be able to move!"

Marley gazed at the chain with mingled awe and amusement. "It is a whopper, isn't it?" he remarked. "Farewell, Scrooge!

"Marley, no!" cried Scrooge, dashing to Marley's side as the figures approached him with the chain. He threw himself on his knees in front of Marley, clinging to him and looking up at him beseechingly. "Help me, Marley! I beg you! Don't let them do this! Marley!'' he babbled.

The four figures surrounded him and began to drape the chain round his arms and legs.

Scrooge clung stubbornly to Marley, crying out in anguish, ''Help me! Marley!''

''Bah! Humbug!'' replied his former partner, quite unmoved. ''Merry Christmas!''

CHAPTER 6.—A NEW MAN.

Heavily tangled in sheets and blankets, Scrooge was clinging grimly to a bedpost at the foot of his bed, fighting to free himself. Desperately he cried out, "Help me! Marley! Please, I beg you!"

He opened his eyes. Bright sunlight was streaming into the room through the wide-open windows through which he had lately flown with the Ghost of Christmas Yet To Come. Scrooge went on struggling with the bedclothes and the bedpost while his sight cleared and his eyes became accustomed to the light.

Gradually he stopped struggling, and leaned, limp and exhausted, against the bedpost, mumbling and groaning to himself. Then he was calm. A great smile dawned across his face as he realized he was safe. "I am alive! I am alive! I've got a chance to change and I will not be the man I was!" he cried in a voice filled with gratitude and reverence. It was as though he realized he was alive for the first time in his life. He looked at the world and the future through different eyes as he sang:

> *I'll begin again.*
> *I will build my life.*
> *I will live to know*
> *That I've fulfilled my life.*
> *I'll begin today,*
> *Throw away the past.*
> *And the future I build*
> *Will be something that will last.*
>
> *I will take the time*
> *I have left to live,*
> *And I'll give it all*
> *That I have left to give.*
> *I will live my days*
> *For my fellow men,*
> *And I'll live in praise*
> *Of the moment when*
> *I was able*
> *To begin again.*
>
> *I will start anew.*
> *I will make amends.*
> *And I'll make quite certain*

That the story ends
On a note of hope
On a strong amen.
And I'll thank the world
And remember when
I was able
To begin again.

Scrooge wandered around his lodgings in a happy daze as he sang, appreciating as never before everything he saw and touched. His happiness bubbled over into impromptu bursts of laughter and improvised jigs and fandangoes. He went over to his desk and threw the tidily stacked papers gleefully up into the air. "I don't know what to do. I'm as light as a feather. I'm as happy as an angel. I'm as giddy as a drunken man. A Merry Christmas, everybody," he cried. "Oh, Jacob Marley, wherever you are, you shall see a change in me, I swear." Then he skipped out of the room, fairly dancing for joy.

He slid down the banisters with accomplished panache, capered across the hall, and flung open the front door. He looked out at the world and the morning sky—a new man.

As Scrooge stood beaming out of his front door, a small boy came trudging through the snow along the alleyway.

"Boy . . . boy . . . boy . . . boy!" Scrooge called to him. "What day is it?"

"Today?"

"Today!"

"Why Christmas Day, o'course!" came the reply.

Scrooge let out a bellow of triumph and clapped his hands. "Christmas Day!" he shouted. "I haven't missed it! The Spirits have done it all in one night! Well they can do anything they like, you see. Of course they can. Of course they can, my fine young fellow." He was beside himself with excitement.

"Now look here, my dear young lad," he continued, "do you know the butcher's shop in the next street but one, on the corner of Cheapside?"

"I should 'ope so!"

"What an intelligent boy! A remarkable boy!" cried Scrooge. "Do you happen to know whether they've sold the prize turkey that was hanging up in the window? Not the big one—the enormous one!"

"You mean the one as big as me?"

"What a delightful boy! So witty! It's a pleasure to talk to him!" exclaimed Scrooge. "That's the one!"

"It's still there!" vouchsafed the child.

"It is? Ha, ha! Go and buy it!"

"Wassat?"

"Go and wake up the butcher and have him open up his shop. Meet me there in ten minutes and I'll give you a shilling! Be holding that turkey, and I'll give you half a crown!"

The boy disappeared like a shot. Scrooge chuckled. "Lovable boy! How I adore children!" he said to himself.

A few minutes later, a beaming Scrooge emerged from the butcher's shop, accompanied by the boy, who was almost totally obscured by the gigantic turkey he was carrying, which was indeed almost as big as he was.

"I can just see Bob Cratchit's face! It's twice the size of Tiny Tim!" cried Scrooge, admiring the huge turkey. "Come along, dear boy—now we'll open up the toyshop!" They hastened away up the street.

The dumbfounded butcher, still half-asleep, stood in his doorway watching them go. He turned to his young apprentice and asked in disbelief, "That *was* old Scrooge, wasn't it?" And the equally dumbfounded apprentice nodded, open-mouthed!

Scrooge and the small boy proceeded to the toyshop, where the many wonderful toys that Tiny Tim and Kathy had so much admired the day before were still in the window. Scrooge engaged the owner of the toyshop in animated conversation, and the poor man was in a state of shock and semi-somnolence as he watched Scrooge leaping round his shop.

"I'll have that—and some of those, and the hobbyhorse, and some flutes— some trumpets, oh and that doll, and some bows and arrows," cried Scrooge.

"Bows and arrows," echoed the owner faintly.

"Oh, yes," Scrooge went on, "I must have a cricket bat and these and that horse and this piano. . . . I like that, oh, this beautiful coach and several kites and these boats and some of these and I'll have that . . ."

The dazed toyshop owner scurried round gathering up the pieces that Scrooge was choosing with such breathtaking speed. The small boy peered over the top of the giant turkey, wide-eyed with wonder at the miracle he was witnessing.

"Yes, Mr. Scrooge," said the owner.

"And one of these—and two of those—and this and this and that!" said

Scrooge. "Now—how much is all that?"

"I-I-I-I . . ." stammered the owner.

"Never mind," replied Scrooge briskly. "Here's five sovereigns. You can keep the change."

The toyshop owner clutched the counter for support. "Yes, Mr. Scrooge."

"And I shall require the services of several small boys—as you can see, this one is covered in turkey!—to help me transport these delightful objects to their destination! Each boy will receive half a crown!"

The toyshop owner reeled. "Half a—," he stammered, "yes, Mr. Scrooge." Then he asked in a dazed voice, "But, Mr. Scrooge, what's *happened?*"

Scrooge regarded him with a bright smile. "What's *happened?*" he cried. "It's perfectly simple, Pringle. I've discovered that I like life!"

Outside again, passers-by stopped and stared incredulously at the unlikely sight of the despicable Scrooge, looking like an elderly but nonetheless jaunty Pied Piper, leading a procession of gift-laden, laughing children down the middle of the street. The urchins who fell foul of Scrooge at the beginning of our story joined the group as Scrooge swept along the street. So did a few mongrel dogs and a couple of stray cats who sensed they might be onto a good thing!

Scrooge halted his little retinue at every shop whose window offered additional Christmas fare, arousing sleeping shopkeepers and opening up closed shops with great authority as and when he needed to. He conducted swift and effective business with each astonished shopkeeper—for they all knew him well—and with gleaming half-crowns recruited still more passing children to bear the sumptuous new burdens of pineapples, and plum cakes, and chestnuts, and bottles of wine, and flowers, and holly, and mistletoe, and mountains of Christmas decorations glittering and dancing with tinsel.

As they all danced along, Scrooge sang deliriously:

> *I like life! Life likes me!*
> *Life and I fairly fully agree—*
> *Life is fine! Life is good!*
> *'Specially mine,*
> *Which is just as it should be!*
>
> *I like pouring the wine,*
> *And why not?*
> *Life's a pleasure*
> *That I deny not!*

— I like life

I like life! Here and now!
Life and I made a mutual vow!
Till I die,
Life and I
We'll both try to be better somehow!

And if life were a woman,
She would be my wife!
Why?
Because I
Like life!

In the crowd stood Scrooge's nephew and his wife. They looked at one another in ·amazement as they saw Scrooge dancing along surrounded by children, and the nephew exclaimed, "Uncle Ebenezer!"

"Merry Christmas to you, me dear boy, and to your enchanting bride!" cried Scrooge, skipping up to them. "We were just on our way to your house with some presents. Here!" As he spoke, he removed some packages from the gift-laden children and stacked them into the arms of his astonished nephew, grinning at the pretty wife as he did so. "These are for you from an old fool who deeply regrets the Christmases gone-by that he might have shared with you! And *this* is for you, my dear! A sort of belated wedding gift!" With that he handed the last and most elaborate package to his niece.

"Oh, Uncle Ebenezer, thank you!" she cried, kissing him. "Christmas lunch is sharp at three. May we expect you?"

"You may! I'll be there! My word, you *are* a pretty girl!" Scrooge chuckled and danced away.

And from behind the enormous pile of packages, his nephew gasped, "I just don't believe it!"

As they passed a clothier's shop, Scrooge spotted a Santa Claus suit in the middle of the window. His eyes twinkled with mischief as he said to himself, "I wonder if I dare!" He moved closer to the window. When he saw himself reflected in the glass it looked as if he was actually dressed as Santa Claus. The smile broadened on his face, and he went into the shop.

A few minutes later he emerged, resplendent in the Santa Claus outfit. The children gave him a mighty roar of approval. With a huge sack of presents, he climbed onto a sleigh, and the children pulled him along the street. And they sang:

Father Christmas! Father Christmas!
He's the greatest man
In the whole wide world!
In the whole wide world!
And he knows it!

Every Christmas
Father Christmas
Puts a great big sack
On his dear ole back
Cos he loves us all
And he shows it!

And he goes

For a sleigh-ride.
If it snows,
Then he may ride all night!
But that's all right!

In the morning—
Christmas morning—
If you lift your eyes,
There's a big surprise!
On your bed you'll see
There's a gift from Father Christmas
From Father Christmas
That's how Christmas ought to be!

When they reached Bob Cratchit's house, Scrooge was still wearing the Santa Claus outfit and obviously loving every minute of it. With the heavy white whiskers and beard, and the unaccustomed twinkle in his eye, he was totally unrecognizable as he jingled merrily away at the little bell by the Cratchit's front door. Deployed around him was the small army of children hidden beneath their Christmas camouflage.

Bob Cratchit opened the door, and his jaw dropped open when he saw Scrooge and his followers. But he did not have the slightest idea that his employer was standing before him.

"Mr. Cratchit? Mr. Robert Cratchit?" inquired Scrooge.

Bob nodded dumbly.

"A Merry Christmas to you, sir, from Santa Claus himself!"

"I think you've got the wrong house!"

"If you are Mr. Robert Cratchit, sir, we've got the right house! Come along, children!" Scrooge swept Bob aside, and the children surged after him into the parlour.

The Cratchit children stood rooted to the spot with amazement watching the bountiful invasion of the family parlour.

Mrs. Cratchit, proudly carrying the overstuffed scrawny goose on a pewter platter, dropped it with a clatter and a cry as she entered the room and beheld Scrooge as Santa Claus and the mountains of gifts already heaped around the room. She looked around nervously for her husband. "Bob?"

Bob's face appeared from behind a holly bush. "It's all right, dear," he said weakly. "We've got—er—visitors."

"Don't worry about your goose, Mrs. Cratchit," Scrooge reassured her briskly. "You can use it as stuffing for this!" With that he dumped the giant turkey into her arms, nearly knocking her off her feet.

Scrooge showered gifts on the four eldest Cratchit children, including the doll for Kathy which she had particularly admired in the toyshop. Then he presented the dumbfounded parents with two heavy leather purses jingling with gold sovereigns. The Cratchits were flabbergasted.

Scrooge chuckled and rubbed his hands gleefully. "Well, I must leave you now," he said. "As you may imagine, this is an extremely busy day for me, and I have many other calls to make!" He turned to go.

Tiny Tim was the only member of the family who had not received a present, but he was far too disappointed to say a word. Then Scrooge turned back and knelt down in front of the little boy. Looking at him tenderly, he exclaimed, "Oh, I almost forgot. This is for you!" With that, he placed the last and largest of the packages on the floor in front of Tiny Tim and lifted off the wrapping. There stood the carousel from the toyshop window—a present beyond Tim's wildest dreams!

"You didn't steal it, did you?" he asked, practical in spite of his happiness.

"No, I didn't steal it!" replied Scrooge with a chuckle. "It's a *present!* For *you!* To keep! A Merry Christmas, Tiny Tim." Gently, he kissed the child on the cheek.

Then he bounced back to his feet, grinning from ear to ear. "You still don't recognize me, do you, Bob Cratchit?" he asked.

"Yes, no—I mean—you're Father Christmas!" stammered Bob.

Scrooge was delighted. He threw back his head and fairly roared with laughter, then with a flourish he removed his false beard and whiskers.

Bob staggered back against the parlour table, and his wife shrieked, "It's Mr. Scrooge! He's gone mad!"

"It's all right, dear," said Bob faintly. "There's nothing to be frightened of!"

"No, I haven't gone mad!" chuckled Scrooge. "And on Monday, when your salary will be doubled—"

"Doubled! He has gone mad!" exclaimed poor Bob.

". . . we'll sit together and discuss what I can do to help your family," Scrooge went on. "To start with, we'll find the right doctors to get young Tiny Tim well. And we *will* get him well, you know, Bob!"

Bob nodded feebly and stammered, "Yes . . . I believe you. . . . I believe anything. . . ."

"And may this be the merriest Christmas of all our lives!" cried Scrooge.

And then he was gone, leaving a stunned silence behind him. The Cratchits looked at one another, and at the heaps of presents, in speechless wonderment. Bob was the first to recover. He spoke slowly, weighing his words carefully. "I don't understand it, I didn't ask for it, but I do believe in good, so I'll be damned if I'm going to argue with it! A Merry Christmas to us all!"

And Tiny Tim said, "God bless us, every one!"

Bob opened wide his arms to embrace his wife, and with cries of delight the little Cratchits ran to the door to see Father Christmas on his merry Christmas way.

As Scrooge danced out of the Cratchit's front door, he spied Tom Jenkins and the two elderly ladies in the crowd. "Tom Jenkins, Tom Jenkins," he called out. "About that six pounds you owe me!"

"You agreed to a few more days, Mr. Scrooge," stammered Tom. "I just need—"

"You can keep it! It's my Christmas present to you!"

"Oh, God bless you this Christmas Day, Mr. Scrooge. Thank you very much!" cried the grateful Tom. Then he began to sing:

Thank you very much!
Thank you very much!
That's the nicest thing
That anyone's ever done for me!

And Scrooge joined in:

It sounds a bit bizarre
But things the way they are
I feel as if another life's
Begun for me!

"And that goes for anybody else who owes me money," cried Scrooge. "You can keep it. . . . As of this day all my debts are ended!" As he spoke he brandished his little black book; then he tore out all the pages and threw them away. The crowd gave a great cheer, and they all went cavorting off down the street, singing and dancing.

There was Scrooge, dancing with the two old ladies who had been his debtors, as if they had been friends all their lives! His bad old self was quite forgotten, as if he really had been dead and buried. He was no longer all alone, for he found himself surrounded by a host of new friends. People were no longer a source of annoyance to him, and everything seemed suddenly brighter. And all the people who had feared him found that old Scrooge was human after all. Everyone was so happy that they just had to sing and dance for all they were worth! And Scrooge was the happiest of all!

As they all danced along, Scrooge noticed the two gentlemen who had been collecting for charity the previous day, and to their amazement he promised them a hundred guineas for their most worthy cause on Monday morning, and the same every Christmas!

The Christmas morning service had just ended, and the congregation was coming out of church as Scrooge and his parade came prancing merrily round the corner into the square. The choir was singing a Christmas carol, and Scrooge's companions were still lustily singing "Thank You Very Much," so there was some confusion as the two groups mingled together.

But when their carol ended, the choirboys saw that those in Scrooge's party were having much more fun than they were. They surged down the church steps, almost trampling the choirmaster underfoot in their eagerness to join the parade. And the other children cascaded after them into the square to fall in behind Scrooge.

The two groups joined together into one big, laughing throng, and Scrooge was the very personification of the spirit of Christmas as he skipped and danced along at the head of the crowd, still dressed as Santa Claus. He was having more fun than he had ever had in his life before as he led his new friends in triumphant procession round the statue in the middle of the square and then away down the street. And everyone sang again:

Thank you very much!
Thank you very much!
That's the nicest thing
That anyone's ever done for me!
It may sound Double Dutch!
But my delight is such
I feel as if a losing war's
Been won for me!

And if I had a flag
I'd hang my flag out—
To add a sort of final victory touch!
But since I left my flag at home
I'll simply have to say
Thank you very, very, very much!

Thank you very much!
Thank you very much!
That's the nicest thing
That anyone's ever done for me!
The future looks all right!
In fact it looks so bright
I feel as if
They're polishing the sun for me!

And if I had a drum
I'd have to bang it!
To add a sort of rumpty tumpty touch!
But since I left my drummer at home!

I'll simply have to say
Thank you very, very, very much!
Thank you very, very, very much!

When they reached the alleyway leading to Scrooge's lodgings, Scrooge bade them farewell with a low bow. Then he turned and skipped happily up to his own front door, leaving the crowd behind.

He took out his keys and let himself in. As he opened the door, he paused to look at the gargoyle doorknocker, then smiled reflectively.

"Hallo!" he said. "I don't know whether you can hear me, Old Jacob Marley, and I don't know whether or not I imagined the things I thought I saw . . . but between the pair of us we finally made a Merry Christmas, didn't we?" Then he went on, "I have to leave you now. I've got to go and get ready. I'm going to spend Christmas with my family." He faltered a little over the last words, which were still rather unfamiliar to him, but he spoke so proudly and happily.

With that he took off his Santa Claus hat and beard. He perched the hat at a jaunty angle on the gargoyle's head and stuck the beard on its chin. Then he gave it an affectionate pat on the nose and went into the house.

As the door closed behind him, the gargoyle's face once again turned into the face of Jacob Marley. His eyes looked up at the Santa Claus hat on his head, and down to the beard on his chin. His customary frown melted and broadened into a happy smile.

And from far away came the echoes of the Christmas carol:

Sing a song of gladness and cheer
For the time of Christmas is here!
Look around about you and see
What a world of wonder
This world can be!

Sing a Christmas carol—
Sing a Christmas carol—
Sing a Christmas carol—
Like the children do!

And enjoy the beauty—
All the joy and beauty—
That a Merry Christmas
Can bring to you!